Barefoot Mud

On The Marble

Written By Nikkie Maud

For my Mum.

Through the marble and the mud, you have always been the

'unbroken songline.'

Thank you for your strength, for your resilience through the storms and for

showing me that even when the world feels disconnected, love is the vibration

that brings us home.

This is for you

Barefoot Mud on the Marble

First Edition: January 2026

Published by Keystrokes by MAUD

ISBN: 9781764056540

Prelude

The Way Of The Snake

A memory shimmered at the edge of Jinjarli's awareness. It was as clear and bright as the rising sun now breaching the horizon. It was seven months ago. In a different season. The air was filled with the dry, dusty scent of late summer, as Jinjarli had been walking a dirt track with his elder, Uncle Keerray. Ochre dust clung to their bare feet and turned their skin the colour of the land. The sun's searing heat was unforgiving on their backs as they dawdled along the winding path. To their left, the jagged peaks of Mount Scoria rose majestically, wearing purple hues. They appeared hazy in the heat.

Uncle Keerray moved at a slow but steady pace. His hand rested lightly on Jinjarli's for balance. Cicadas screamed a high-pitched song that filled the air and dry leaves broke with a crisp crunch underfoot. Keerray paused and his grip tightened slightly on Jinjarli's arm. He pointed towards the distant kangaroo grass: it was moving in just one section, a subtle undulation against the stillness.

"Let old Unc tell you about that snake there, right?" the Elder began, his voice dry like the grass. "That old snake, he was movin' through the kangaroo grass, eh? The sun was beatin' down, making the dirt shimmer. He wasn't in any hurry, just taking his time, feeling the warmth of the ground. You could see him slitherin', low to the earth, his body long and strong. As he went, you'd see little bits of that dry sand and those tiny stones there flick up behind him this way and that. Like the ground was breathin' as he passed."

Jinjarli watched, mesmerised by the hypnotic movement.

"Sometimes, when the ground got a bit rougher, with those sharp little rocks sticking out, he'd crawl himself up. Not fast, mind you, but steady. You'd still see him flicking up bits of that hard ground as he pushed himself along, looking for a cool spot under a rock or maybe a juicy little lizard for a feed. Other times, when the ground was smoother, maybe just after a bit of rain had settled the dust, he'd glide along. Smooth as water over stone, he'd move. Even then, you'd see him flick up the lightest dust. A whisper on the land. The way his body moved, that up and down, side to side, that's how he got through the bush." The Elder turned to Jinjarli, his eyes shining with an intensity that defied his age and nodded with certainty.

"That's the way of the snake, nephew. Always movin', always touchin' the land. You watch closely now. The land tells you the story, even in the little things he flicks up along the way. You watch. Do you see that old snake slitherin' through the grass? He's been movin' across this ground for longer than you can imagine. Just like his ancestors have been movin' here, the Gundarra people have walked this country for more than sixty-five thousand years. That's a long, long time. Think about it. That's more seasons than there are stars in the sky on the clearest night.

"Our old people were here when the mountains were shaped differently, when the rivers flowed in different directions. They watched the giant creatures roam this land, creatures that are now just stories and bones in the ground. They learned the language of the land, the whispers of the wind through the Kangaroo Grass and the stories told by the rustling of the Spear Grass. They knew shelter was given by the Tussock. They knew when the bush fruits were ripe, where to find the cool water and how the animals moved with the changin' seasons." Uncle Keerray paused, looking back at the snake, now just a ripple in the distance.

"Every footprint we left on this earth, every story we painted on the rocks, nephew, every song we sang under the stars, it all connects us to this place. That snake, he feels the spirit of this land through his body when he moves across the land, just like we do in our hearts when we touch Country. He's part of the same story, a story that stretches back through all those thousands of years. Our ancestors walked this land. They hunted on this land and raised their families on this land. Their spirits are in the rocks and the waterholes, even in the air we breathe. When we walk on Country, we walk with them. When we listen to the wind in the grass, we hear their voices.

So, when you see that snake there movin', remember he's not just movin' now. He's carryin' the memory of all the snakes that came before him, just like we carry the memory of all our old people." Uncle Keerray paused for a moment and looked at Jinjarli knowingly before he continued.

"This land – Gundarra Country – holds our story. A story that has been here since the start of time. It's a story that's still being told with every sunrise and every step we take on this dusty ground. We are here to look after this land. Remember that and you will go far."

His voice trailed off as they continued around the outside of the sleeping volcano. Jinjarli had always listened with full attention when his elders spoke. It wasn't just out of respect; he knew their words held ancient wisdom. Codes for survival were hidden in simple stories about snakes.

. . . .

As the memory faded, Jinjarli's awareness returned to the studio. He looked at a large, half-finished canvas awaiting his return. It was meant to be a depiction of the snake from Uncle Keerray's story, moving through the grass. Jinjarli picked up his palette, the wood stained with layers of old paint. He squeezed out a dollop of yellow ochre then a blob of burnt sienna. He picked up his brush and dipped it into the medium. The smell of the chemicals hit the back of his throat. He stared at the canvas. Usually, this was his moment of flow. The moment where his hand became an extension of his spirit, where the brush was just a conduit for the story. Today, his arm felt like lead. It felt heavy, disconnected from his heart. It felt as if the connection between his mind and his hand had been severed, blocked by the static in his head.

He made a mark on the canvas. A sweep of yellow meant to represent the dry grass. It didn't whisper; it shouted. It was a heavy, lifeless slab of acrylic plastic sitting dormant on the cotton weave. There was no 'flick'. Uncle Keerray had said the snake moved like water over stone, leaving a trail of light dust. Jinjarli tried to replicate that delicate glide; his wrist was locked, stiffened by the invisible weight pressing on his shoulders. Instead of a glide, the brush dragged through the medium like a plough through wet cement. He mixed a darker brown for the shadow, trying to find the rhythm. His hand refused to dance. It stuttered. The mark he made wasn't a snake; it was a slug, heavy, static and stuck. He pushed the paint around, bullying it, trying to force movement where there was none; his touch was clumsy, cut-off from source. The mud in his head had travelled down his arm, turning his fine motor skills into blunt instruments. Jinjarli forced the brush, his grip tightening until his knuckles turned white. He was trying to manufacture the feeling, trying to replicate the sensation of the snake, but the interference was too loud and the paint just became muddy.

Chapter 1

The Rubber Coffins

Jinjarli was a young Gundarra man and an artist. For weeks, a debilitating sluggishness had clouded his mind and made his limbs feel like lead, leaving his vibrant ochre paintings dead and flat in his Hammaholl art studio. Uncle Keerray taught him this wasn't mere stress. It was the physical consequence of the concrete wall built between his feet and the pulse of the Earth. Jinjarli was determined to heal. He started his days with a trip out of town to touch base with Country. It was nearing the end of winter and the dark, damp earth welcomed the young man's bare feet, a sensation that was less of a touch and more of an embrace. It wasn't just soft; it was cold, a deep, shocking coolness that surged up from the soles of his feet. It instantly chased away the sluggish residue of his restless night. Jinjarli sank slightly into the top layer of soil, feeling the fine, gritty dust give way to the smooth, almost slick texture of the overnight dew. This was his ancestral land and his feet knew its language intimately. They knew the difference between the sharp bite of granite sand and the forgiving yield of river silt without him even looking down. He smiled and felt at home instantly.

He gazed over to the eastern edge of Lake Lumina. It was lined with the big, old river gums that stretched out and up towards the sky. Their bark was peeling in long, grey strips, revealing the smooth, salmon-coloured flesh underneath. They were ghost-like in the pre-dawn obscurity. Through the twisted and tangled branches, the first hesitant spears of sunlight poked through. The light wasn't harsh yet; it was gentle and golden, painting stripes across the young man's face, making the fine hairs on his skin stand on end. Mist still clung to the sleeping water, like a soft, white blanket, reluctant to be pulled away by the increasing light. It swirled in slow, lazy eddies, mimicking the dreamtime spirits that Uncle Keerray said still danced when the world was quiet. As it slowly lifted, it revealed patches of dark, still water where the first light shimmered. The lake's surface was as smooth as polished stone, holding the morning's secrets close.

The air felt cool on Jinjarli's skin. It carried the damp scent of the earth still waking up. He took a deep, exaggerated breath. He held the air in his lungs as if he could filter the nutrients from it directly into his blood. The primal aroma of Country, a complex perfume of wet bark, cool soil, the sharp medicinal aroma of eucalyptus oil released in the morning humidity and the sweet decay of fallen gum leaves. It was as familiar and comforting as Grandmother's hugs. It was a smell that bypassed the brain and went straight to the heartstrings. The sound of the urban world was absent out here. There were no engines, no sirens and no hum of electricity.

Instead, a chorus of waking magpies sang their morning greetings. The calls echoed across the landscape, a complex, fluting melody that sounded like water tumbling over rocks. This was nature's own alarm clock, a song that had been sung in this exact spot for millennia. The birdsong was accompanied by the softest lap of water against the shore, a rhythmic hushing sound and the sleepy, cadence croaking of a Pobblebonk frog hidden deep in the reeds. It sounded like a banjo string being plucked underwater.

The man started to move through the dewy grass. Each slow, deliberate step was a quiet greeting to the earth, the moisture soaking into his skin, turning the dust on his feet into a thin layer of mud. A little shiver ran through him. It reminded him of the night just past. He paused for a moment, looking out over the lake. In the distance, Mount Scoria was a giant silhouette, a familiar and comforting shape against the brightening sky. It sat heavy on the horizon, a dormant guardian that had watched over his people since the fires burned inside it. Another day, Jinjarli thought, a tiny sigh escaping his lips. He swallowed, tasting the fresh, moist air again. Walking here and feeling the earth underfoot brought a sense of calm, a quiet strength that the town couldn't offer. He needed it. For weeks, a heavy cloak of exhaustion had been his constant companion. It wasn't just physical tiredness; it was a spiritual gravity. He felt like a radio tuned slightly off-station, receiving only static where there should be music.

The whispers of the wind, high in the gum trees, spoke, rustling the leaves like dry paper. This was the language he had known since childhood, a feeling more than words. 'Funny how things change, but some things stay the same,' Jinjarli mused, watching a dragonfly dart across the water. Two hundred and thirty-five years. A long time to be pushed and pulled, to have your world shrink, to have fences put up across the songlines. A kookaburra let out a laugh from the high branch of a gum, a raucous, mocking sound that broke the magnificence of the morning. A lizard darted off a rock and out of sight, a flash of skittering movement. Jinjarli recalled his elder, Uncle Keerray's words, spoken by the fire only a few nights before, You walk on the hard ground, yes, but you don't feel it. You wear the rubber coffins on your feet and wonder why your spirit is dead. The elders, with their fierce love for this land and their endless fighting with words and paper... They had won, hadn't they? A piece of paper from a faraway king, a strange magic, but it meant this land was theirs, a promise against ever being moved again. He felt the weight of that history lift slightly, a profound spiritual relief that came with the sunrise over the land.

A lone pelican stretched its wings with a lazy flap, a massive span of grey and white that settled onto the water and sent out gentle ripples that echoed all the way to the water's edge. He turned and headed back towards town. He reached the boundary line. The old wire fence marked the end of the reserve and the beginning of town. This was the threshold. The transition point between the world that breathed and the world that held its breath. He stopped at the edge of the asphalt. He looked down at his bare feet, brown and dusted with the sacred soil of the lake bank. With an almost physical reluctance, he dropped his backpack to the ground and pulled out his runners. They were cheap, mass-produced things with thick white rubber soles. As he slid his feet into them, he felt an immediate, suffocating separation. It was like putting on a blindfold, but for his soles. The intricate data of the ground, the temperature, the texture and the subtle vibration of the earth were instantly cut off, replaced by the flat, spongy indifference of a synthetic insole. He tied the laces. It felt like he was sealing a contract he didn't want to sign.

He stepped onto the pavement. The sensation was jarring. The asphalt was hard, unforgiving, dead. Even at this early hour, it held a radiant, unnatural heat, a memory of yesterday's sun trapped in the bitumen. The shock travelled up his shins, a dull impact with every step that his body wasn't designed to absorb. It was a rhythmic jarring, thud that echoed in his knees and hips. As he walked deeper into Hammaholl, the sickness began to creep in. It wasn't just a mental shift; it was a physiological assault. The song of the magpies was replaced by the low-frequency hum of the electrical substation on the corner, a sound that seemed to vibrate in his teeth like a trapped blowfly. A rubbish truck groaned in the distance, its hydraulic whine cutting through the morning air like a rusty saw, followed by the crash of glass bottles being dumped. The air changed, too. The sweet scent of eucalyptus and damp earth was choked out by the metallic gassiness of car exhaust and the claustrophobic smell of old frying oil venting from a bakery preparing for the morning rush.

Jinjarli walked past rows of suburban houses, each one a brick-veneer fortress, isolated from the next. He slowed as he passed number 42. Mr Henderson was out in the driveway, hosing down his blue Toyota. Henderson was wearing green gumboots, standing on the concrete, washing a machine of rubber and steel with a yellow sponge. The chemical tang of fake-lemon car wash cut through the air, stinging Jinjarli's nose. Henderson looked up, the hose dripping in his hand. His face was grey and sagging, eyes rimmed with red, looking just as tired as Jinjarli had felt an hour ago.

"Morning," Henderson grunted, barely shifting his gaze.

"Morning," Jinjarli replied, keeping his pace. He wanted to ask, Do you feel it? The buzz? The wall? But he saw the exhaustion etched into the older man's posture. Henderson was standing on the earth, but he was floating in rubber, severed from the source. A ghost in his own driveway.

Jinjarli felt the isolation keenly. He was walking through a purgatory of straight lines and hard surfaces, a world designed to keep the human spirit isolated. By the time he reached the door of his studio, the peace of the sunrise felt like a dream he had already forgotten. The clarity of the sunrise over

Lake Lumina faded completely, abruptly replaced by the familiar, low-level buzz of fluorescent lights as he flicked the switch in his studio. The quiet, rhythmic sound was the relentless hum of the town's mechanical world, a jarring, artificial presence that immediately smothered the morning's peace. The atmosphere was pungent with the turpentine and linseed oil that perpetually gripped the air in Jinjarli's Hammaholl studio. It was a smell he used to love, the smell of creation, but lately, it just smelled like struggle.

He dropped his keys on the bench, a loud clang in the quiet room, then went to open the window. He pushed the sash up, desperate for a breeze. The air that drifted in was stale, carrying the exhaust of a passing bus. He put the kettle on; morning coffee was a must, a desperate attempt to jump-start a system that felt like it was running on empty. He watched the blue flame of the gas burner, mesmerised by its artificial purity. The water bubbled, then screamed. He poured the water. The steam rose up. It didn't smell like the steam of a campfire. It smelled of chlorine and copper pipes.

The vibrant energy of the dawn was leaching away as the day began demanding its due. Canvases leant against the walls, their surfaces bearing the ghosts of abandoned ideas. He walked past them, his eyes critical and tired. There was a painting of the river he had started two weeks ago. It was technically good; the perspective was right and the colours were mixed correctly, but it felt dead. It was a picture of the river, not the spirit of the river. It lacked the pulse. He moved to his easel. There was a physical pressure that obscured his vision. He felt disconnected not just from the earth but from his own talent. The paint just sat there, stubborn. It was coloured mud and felt like it was mocking him.

"Come on," he whispered, grit in his voice. "Flow. Where are you?" He slashed at the canvas, a jagged line that ruined the curve he had spent hours on yesterday. It was an ugly mark, a mark of frustration. He dropped the brush. It clattered onto the wooden floor, rolling under the table, leaving a smear of brown paint on the floorboards. Frustration gnawed at the edges of his focus. It was another morning lost to the persistent drag, another attempt at capturing the spirit of the land on canvas, derailed by the weight of sluggishness. It was as if the rubber soles of his shoes had grown over his soul, insulating him from the very source of his art.

He ran a hand through his almost black hair, pulling at the roots, trying to wake up his scalp. The movement was slow and reluctant. He felt trapped in the square room, trapped by the walls, trapped by the buzzing lights that flickered with a frequency that made his eyes ache. He paced the room. Four steps to the window. Four steps back. A cage. He looked at the other paintings: landscapes, portraits of elders and abstract patterns. They all seemed to stare back at him, accusing him of losing the thread. 'You are painting the surface,' they seemed to say. You have forgotten what lies beneath. His gaze fell upon a chunk of basalt resting on a nearby table. It was a dense, dark piece that he had brought back from a recent walk up Mount Scoria. It sat there, heavy and silent, a piece of the mountain brought indoors. He had intended to incorporate its rough texture into a sculpture, a physical form that might embody the quiet strength of the stone, but he hadn't touched it in days. Almost unconsciously, Jinjarli's fingers reached out. He needed something real. Something that wasn't plastic or paint or concrete or processed wood. He needed something that remembered the fire that made it. He traced the cool, uneven surface of the basalt. It was rough against his fingertips, pitted with tiny holes where ancient gas bubbles had escaped the lava millions of years ago. A momentary stillness settled over him. It was instant. As his skin touched the rock, the persistent grasp of fatigue eased faintly; it was almost imperceptible. It was fleeting, a whisper of calm in the storm of his mind. Yet, it sparked a flicker of something... curiosity? Recognition? The feeling was similar to the quiet strength he found by the lake each morning, a subtle resonance with the earth itself. It was a feeling that went deeper than just intuition. It was a circuit closing. Jinjarli stood there, his hand on the rock, his breathing slowed down. He didn't have the words for it yet. All he knew was that for the first time since he put his shoes on that morning, the noise in his head had dialled down, just a fraction and in that silence, he began to wonder.

Chapter 2

The Antiseptic Vacuum

Later that morning an appointment with the local GP had Jinjarli walking through the sliding door of the Hammaholl Medical Centre. The door hissed shut behind him. It sounded so final and air-tight. He felt like he had stepped into a vacuum chamber. The fresh air outside was out played by the thin, aggressive scent of antiseptic, a smell that promised hygiene but delivered anxiety. Jinjarli stood in the foyer for a moment. The air didn't flow; it vibrated. It was a hermetically sealed box where the atmosphere had been scrubbed, filtered and recirculated so many times it tasted like recycled plastic. He took a shallow breath; the smell hit him instantly: the lung-stuffing, chemical bouquet of clean. It was a cocktail of industrial-strength floor polish, ethanol-based hand sanitiser and the faint smell of heating elements burning off dust. It coated the back of his throat, a taste that was simultaneously sweet and metallic.

Above him, the fluorescent lights hummed with a manic energy. It wasn't a sound you heard with your ears so much as felt in your teeth, a high-frequency mosquito whine that drilled straight into the base of the skull. Jinjarli squinted. The light wasn't the warm, golden spectrum of the sun; it was a blue-white strobe, flickering just fast enough to be invisible to the eye but exhausting to the brain. It flattened everything it touched, turning the patient's skin sallow and the plastic chairs a sickly shade of grey. This building was designed to keep nature out, but in doing so, it had created a barrier. There were no negative ions here, no fresh electrons from the earth. Just a build-up of positive static charge that clung to your clothes and made your hair stand on end. Jinjarli looked at a potted plant in the corner, a peace lily with brown, crispy edges, slowly dying under the artificial glare. I know how you feel, little one, he thought. We are both drying out in here.

He entered the waiting room; the walls were painted a non-committal, institutional white, adorned only with framed, abstract prints of landscapes, all colour and movement smoothed out into something sterile and safe. The effect was suffocating. Jinjarli found himself instinctively rubbing the soles of his feet together, a silent, desperate attempt to feel the rough, cool texture of the earth beneath the layers of lino and concrete. He located the only vacant seat against the back wall, moulded from unforgiving, cold plastic. He sank into it. The material immediately conducted the building's chill into Jinjarli's muscles. He wasn't alone. The occupants were scattered across the plastic chairs, each one a tiny, isolated island in a sea of shared, silent malaise. He settled in and began to observe, his artist's eye cataloguing the details of human tiredness around him.

Near the magazine rack sat an elderly woman, dressed in a faded, purple cardigan. Her face was a map of persistent discomfort. She wasn't reading; she was merely staring at the clock, occasionally emitting a soft, deep sigh that seemed to deflate her entire body. Her foot, swollen slightly at the ankle, rested on a small, worn cushion she had obviously brought herself. She was a fixture here, her body broken, not by sudden trauma, but by the relentless, decades-long disconnect from the natural world. She was the quiet symbol of the modern system's failure to cure, only to manage.

Across the room, a big, restless man in paint-splattered jeans, a tradie, clearly, was attempting to read a 2-year-old copy of Australian Geographic. His foot relentlessly tapped the floor, the sound a low, rhythmic thump-thump-thump that grated on Jinjarli's nerves. His hands were thick and calloused, hands meant for working with wood and earth, yet they gripped the slick magazine pages with a nervous, unseeing tension. He was the prototype of the modern worker, physically exhausted but mentally wired, unable to slow down. Jinjarli imagined Dr Finch would see him and immediately scribble "Anxiety" and a new prescription for something to dull the edge.

The most dynamic presence in the room was a young mother trying to contain her toddler. The child, about three, was a cyclone of messy energy, the very opposite of the sterile calm the clinic demanded. The little fella, dressed in a bright orange jumper, wasn't sick; he was bored. He yearned for space to run, for the soft give of the earth under his little runners. He ignored the dull plastic toys, preferring to dismantle a tower of oversized wooden blocks. Suddenly, the child swatted the tower. The blocks scattered, clattering loudly across the Lino floor. The sound was shocking in the forced silence; the chronic complainer flinched. The mother, instantly mortified, scrambled to retrieve the toys, her face tightening with a mask of modern stress as she shot apologetic glances at the other patients. Her apology, a sharp hiss,

"Sorry, so sorry," revealed the pervasive fear of public judgement. This small eruption of natural chaos was instantly suppressed by the sterile environment.

Jinjarli's gaze drifted to the oversized wall clock. The minute hand moved with a decisive, mechanical clack that cut through the low whirring of the air conditioner. The second hand was a relentless metronome, counting the waiting time and his dwindling hope. The lost hours of his own creative time. His hand passed across the smooth, unfeeling plastic chair. He found himself thinking of the basalt he had touched earlier in his studio, cool and alive with energy. Here, the plastic was cold and dead. It was an insulator.

The entire building, he realised with a sudden, chilling clarity, was built to insulate the body from the earth and the people inside were suffering the consequence. He had come to the architects of the disconnect, for a cure. It was bloody mad, really. The clock ticked again. His focus turned to the stressed tradie. His anxious tapping suddenly reminded him of the drumbeat of a corroboree, except warped and frantic. He was trying to ground himself, his energy seeking an outlet, but the floor provided none. He was just absorbing the building's static. A finality settled in the air when the inner door creaked open. A nurse, wearing a blue shirt, black pants and a heavily rehearsed smile, stepped out. She moved with an almost unnatural efficiency across the Lino floor, her movements devoid of the natural rhythm found in the bush.

"Dot," she called, her voice bright and impersonal. She proceeded to lead the old lady towards the inner sanctum. Jinjarli let out a loud sigh. He had, of course, anticipated his own name being called. The air in the waiting room felt thin and over-recycled; the metallic, chemical scent assaulted his nostrils. The muted ticking of the wall clock seemed to get louder and amplify the beat of his heart. He had been avoiding this appointment for weeks; the sheer act of being there, sitting in that stiff, unfamiliar quiet, was an acknowledgement of his failure to heal himself. The room was a study in repressed noise and synthetic materials. Jinjarli felt small.

There was another startling crash as the child knocked down another tower. The small chaos unnerved Jinjarli, yet clarified his thoughts. It was the frantic, unnatural pace and stress. Life allowed no space for noise and no outlet for natural energy. He contemplated getting up and simply walking out, succumbing to the urge to flee the sterile silence and return to the breathing earth. But the persistent weariness that had become his shadow held him captive. The inner door creaked open for the second time. The nurse came out again, same blue shirt, same black pants and same heavily rehearsed smile. She moved again with an almost unnatural efficiency across the Lino floor.

"Jinjarli," she called, her voice again bright and impersonal. Jinjarli followed her back through the door and into the doctor's room.

Dr Finch was a figure of absolute clinical certainty. His neatly trimmed beard and crisp white coat echoed the order and authority of his position. He sat behind a large oak desk. His gaze was fixed on the notes in front of him; he didn't look up immediately. The delay stretched. It was deliberate and established the doctor's dominion over the temporal and professional space. Jinjarli settled into the empty leather armchair. He watched the doctor's profile, noticing a small scar on the bridge of his nose, a jagged line that seemed entirely out of place on his otherwise flawless face. The doctor's hands were perfectly still, a chilling contrast to the nervous twitch Jinjarli felt in his own fingers. A low, rhythmic tick of a clock on the wall was the only sound. The thin paper of the notes rustled faintly as the doctor turned a page, the sound surprisingly loud and intrusive in the sterile stillness. Jinjarli's gaze drifted from the doctor's composed face to the imposing oak desk, so grand it seemed to absorb the light. The room smelled sharply of antiseptic and conditioned leather, a smell as foreign to Jinjarli as the sterile silence. He felt small in the leather armchair; its coolness even felt manufactured.

Dr Finch was a man of his own world, a world of crisp lines, precise numbers and written words that held far more power than a spoken promise. Jinjarli wondered what those notes truly said about him, a life measured in clinical observations instead of the stories of his family, the taste of fire-cooked goanna or the feel of ancient river stones under his bare feet. He shifted in the armchair, the leather giving a loud squeak that was an intruder in the awkward stillness. All he could do was wait for the verdict, held captive by the quiet authority of a man who hadn't even looked up at him.

"So, Jinjarli," the Doctor began at last, his voice a measured baritone, finally raising his eyes. "You've been experiencing persistent fatigue?" Jinjarli nodded, the weight of his weariness feeling almost physical.

"Yes, Doctor. For weeks now. It's more than just being tired. It's, I don't know... a heaviness, like I'm wading through mud all the time. My head feels foggy and..." He tried to articulate the deeper unease, the feeling that this was not just the usual ebb and flow of energy: "...It feels... disconnected, somehow." He finished, the phrase sounding small and fragile against the walls of logic. Dr Finch's expression was polite but faintly dismissive.

"Disconnected? Perhaps you've been under a bit of stress? Work, personal life... anything out of the ordinary?" He tapped his pen against the notes. "It's quite common, especially with the pace of modern life." Jinjarli hesitated. The words about a subtle energy from the earth felt foolish under the doctor's clinical gaze.

"I'm an artist," he said instead. "Sometimes there are deadlines... but this feels different. It's... in my bones."

Finch looked at the young man's hands. They were stained with ochre and dirt. To Jinjarli, that dirt was culture. To Finch, it was a vector. In his mind's eye, he didn't see a connection; he saw microbes. He saw tetanus spores living in the dust, hookworm larvae waiting in the mud and the chaotic, microscopic violence of the natural world that humanity had spent five thousand years building walls to keep out. He wasn't trying to oppress this boy; he was trying to sanitise him. To Finch, the disconnect wasn't a sickness; it was the sterile shield of civilisation, the only thing standing between order and the rot of sepsis.

"Well," Dr Finch concluded, leaning back in his chair, his tone suggesting the matter was already settled. "It certainly sounds like stress manifesting physically. We see a lot of that. The body has its

ways of telling us to slow down." He reached for a prescription pad.

"I'm going to prescribe you a mild antidepressant. It can often help regulate energy levels and improve overall well-being. Take one tablet daily, preferably in the morning and with food. Try to get more rest, perhaps some light exercise." He tore off the prescription and handed it across the desk, his gaze already gone back to his notes. "Come back in a month if things haven't improved."

Jinjarli stared at the slip of paper in his hand. The neat, official script was a stark contrast to the intuitive knowing that stirred within him. Antidepressants. Rest. Exercise. The usual answers. But he hadn't mentioned the persistent buzz beneath his skin when he walked barefoot by the lake or the fleeting sense of clarity when he touched the cool basalt. He had not spoken of Uncle Keerray's ancient words, the whisper of a deeper connection lost. The feeling of being disconnected was not stress. It was something else entirely, something Dr Finch, in his well-lit office, seemed unable or unwilling to see. A seed of doubt, not about his own intuition, but about the limitations of this modern, disconnected approach to healing, took root in Jinjarli's mind. The sterile white of Dr Finch's prescription seemed to blur, the messy letters swimming before Jinjarli's eyes....

. . . .

A voice echoed in his memory, weathered and warm like the sun-baked earth. It was Uncle Keerray. He could almost feel the elder's hand, gnarled like an ancient root, resting gently on his arm as he sat by the crackling fire, the scent of burning gum sharp in the cool evening air.

"You young ones," Keerray had said, his gaze distant, as if peering back through the veils of time. "You walk on the hard ground, yes, but you don't feel it. These..." The elder had gestured down at Jinjarli's own worn leather boots, the everyday armour against the modern world. "...these keep you separate. Like a wall between your feet and the breathing earth."

A small frown had creased Jinjarli's brow. Separate? They were practical and protective. But Keerray's eyes, though clouded with age, held a sharp knowing.

"Our ancestors, they walked barefoot. They felt the land, its coolness, its warmth, its strength. It was part of them, just as the air they breathed. Now this... grey fatigue... it creeps in. We are meant to touch the earth, young fella. To feel its pulse. When that link is broken..." The elder had trailed off, a deep sadness in his gaze, the unspoken words hanging heavy in the smoky air.

We wither.

Chapter 3

The Secret Knock

A nervous flutter tightened in Jinjarli's chest as he stood on Mr Henderson's porch in Hammaholl Street. The small, elevated space was a physical contradiction to the order he'd just left at the doctor's office. The house was overflowing with tinkering projects and had the faint scent of solder. It was an absolute treasure trove of forgotten gadgets. A halfway house for the things that the rest of society had discarded. Jinjarli felt exposed, standing there with the secret weight of Uncle Keerray's wisdom pressing down on him. He took a slow breath, forcing his voice to remain even and his gestures vague. He couldn't risk exposing his true theory, that the earth had a pulse, to a practical man like Mr Henderson.

"Just need it for... an art project, Mr Henderson," Jinjarli explained, trying to keep his composure as he gestured vaguely with his hands. He watched the old man's face for any sign of disbelief. "Testing... soil conductivity, you know, for some sculptures I'm planning," he elaborated, attempting to give his story a scientific veneer. Mr Henderson merely grunted, a sound that conveyed volumes of scepticism about art projects but not enough to refuse a simple favour. His eyes twinkled behind his thick glasses as he disappeared into the cluttered garage. The heavy, scraping sound of misplaced tools being shuffled echoed sharply before the old man emerged a few moments later. He carried in his calloused hand a dusty yellow multimeter. The plastic casing was worn and its screen was blank and expectant. It was a tool of pure logic, retrieved from the junk heap, now poised to bridge the gap between ancient belief and quantifiable fact.

"She's been sitting out there for a while," the old tinker said, holding the device out. "You might have to get her a new battery. She'll be as good as gold then," he advised pragmatically. Jinjarli took the dusty multimeter. The cold, hard plastic felt alien yet essential in his hand, a functional contrast to the cool basalt rock he had instinctively touched earlier.

"Thank you, Mr Henderson," Jinjarli replied, his voice barely a whisper. He fled the porch quickly, the yellow meter feeling less like a tool and more like a fragile, crucial artefact of his impending personal revolution.

. . . .

Back in his yard behind the studio, the borrowed multimeter was a hard plastic and felt cold in Jinjarli's hands. The air hung still and heavy. It was thick with the cloying sweetness of jasmine and the raw, earthy scent of damp soil. This was a smell that always pulled at something deep inside Jinjarli, an aroma of country even in this small, fenced-in space. He knelt in the neglected grass. The evening light was low and filtered through the gnarled branches of the old plum tree and onto the overgrown tomato plants. The cracked, sun-bleached concrete patio was lifting against the tenacious weeds. The skeletons of rose bushes from another time lined the boundary of his small, contained yard.

Jinjarli's heart thumped a nervous rhythm against his ribs, a frantic drumbeat in the quiet vastness of his growing theory. Dr Finch's dismissive voice had been smooth and confident. It still echoed in his ears. It was the clinical counterpoint to the deep echoes of Uncle Keerray's ancient wisdom. 'A wall between your feet and the breathing earth.' The phrase was simple yet profound and it clung to him like a teething two-year-old. He took a deep, shaky breath. The dampness from the earth filled his lungs. Hesitantly, Jinjarli pulled up the leg of his worn jeans. His skin now unsheltered from the cool evening air. He felt a gentle tickle as goosebumps spread across the surface of his skin and the tiny hairs all stood to attention. He took another deep breath as he placed the cold metallic tip of the red probe against the warm flesh of his ankle. It felt clinical, like a doctor's touch. Not his own. He followed by pressing the black probe firmly into a patch of dark soil near the struggling tomato plants. The soil was rich and damp. He felt the earth's cool, grainy texture give way, the dampness clinging to the probe's tip. This was not a sterile lab or a clean tile floor. This was the living, breathing and dirty ground.

The multimeter's screen flickered to life. Numbers danced across the dull grey surface, a chaotic, jumbled static that mirrored Jinjarli's racing thoughts. His breath hitched in his throat. He held it. It was a physical pause in a moment that felt like it could actually shatter. Then, the chaos settled. The static gave way to a small, stable reading: 0.03 volts. Jinjarli blinked. The numbers didn't move. He leant closer, the scent of the earth becoming stronger and earthier. He felt the tiniest tremor in the lead connected to the soil. He actually felt the ever so faint pulse of energy. The mini jolt was not a shock from the meter; it was something else entirely, a beat of pure, unadulterated excitement mixed with a breathtaking disbelief.

Could it be that simple?

The logical part of Jinjarli's brain had been conditioned by years of conventional education and the endless chatter of the news. It was screaming at him. This isn't real science, Jinjarli. You're not a scientist. This is just a gimmick. Then he felt a different kind of current. A resonance on his skin. A feeling that went deeper than just a number on a screen. This wasn't just a reading. It was a reply. The earth had spoken, not with a voice of data, but with a pulse. For the first time, Jinjarli felt himself listening. It was the same feeling that surfaced when he walked barefoot by Lake Lumina, or traced his fingers over the rough, healing bark of an old gum tree or when his spirit soared, gazing at the majestic peaks of Mount Scoria. It was the ancestral knowledge his elders had carefully, fearfully, passed down. This tiny number was just confirmation.

To test the counterpoint and to truly confirm, or deny, this audacious possibility, Jinjarli shifted his other foot onto a discarded rubber car mat that he had placed nearby. Its black surface was dull and insulating against the Earth. The probe on his ankle remained fixed. Instantly, the reading vanished, the screen returning to a flat zero. A sharp intake of breath caught in the young man's throat. The air was still thick he tasted the soil and the lingering tang of urban exhaust in the back of his throat. The meter seemed to hold its breath with him. Zero. Then, back in the earth, the reading returned. Again. And again. The numbers, though small, were consistent. When his skin connected with the Earth, there was a measurable electrical potential and when insulated, it disappeared.

The realisation hit Jinjarli like a sudden shockwave sweeping across a desert plain. It wasn't just a feeling. It was an extreme sense of wonder and it stirred deep within him. The weariness that had become his constant company reluctantly stepped aside. It was real. It was tangible. It was a measurable phenomenon. The raw, earthy smell of his backyard, the cool bite of the probes and the stark contrast of the screen all solidified into a single, astounding truth. The Earth was this ancient, living entity and it was a source of energy. A wellspring of something vital that flows into people when they make direct contact with it. The shoes, those modern conveniences, those everyday armours that separated us from the ground, were rubber coffins for the soles. They were indeed a wall.   A surge of exhilarating, almost terrifying, excitement coursed through him. This wasn't just about his own fatigue anymore. This was bigger. This was the severed root Uncle Keerray had spoken of, laid bare by a simple device. 'This is the breathing earth,' the quiet voice within him whispered again, but this time, it was no longer a whisper. It was a deafening chorus. This is the very essence of why our ancestors walked barefoot, why they sat directly on the land and why they built their homes from stone. It's not just culture; it's survival. It's healthcare. The implications stretched out before him. They were vast and overwhelming.

If Jinjarli's tired body and his foggy mind felt even a tiny improvement from this subtle connection, what about others? What about the rampant illnesses, the chronic pains and the sleepless nights so many suffer from in the modern world? A fierce, protective urge, not just for his own people, the Gundarra, but for all of humanity, began to bloom in Jinjarli's heart. It was emotion as powerful as the ancestral pride that surged through his veins. It felt like the true beginning of something extraordinary, a bridge forming between ancient wisdom and a modern scientific reading, a path stretching out from his small backyard into a world hungry for healing. The sun finally dipped below the horizon, painting the sky in a fiery display of orange and violet, as if celebrating Jinjarli's silent revelation.

The air in the yard was giving way to the cool, settling evening. Jinjarli stepped onto the cracked concrete patio, wiping the excess mud from his bare feet on the coarse mat before sliding the glass door of his studio open. The shift was immediate and jarring. The cool, earthy scent of damp soil was immediately overpowered by the turpentine tang and linseed oil that insisted on clinging to the air in the studio. Jinjarli walked past the leaning canvases as the vibrant energy he'd felt outside began to leach away; the familiar, thick weariness, like a shroud, settled over him again. He sighed, feeling the day and the heavy weight of the new discovery demand their due.

He carried the dusty yellow multimeter gently, placing it on his workbench beside the chunk of basalt he had brought back from Mount Scoria. The plastic tool was no longer a gimmick; it was an artefact of proof. Its dull grey screen, which had spoken an undeniable truth, was now blank and reflecting the low-level buzz of the fluorescent lights. Instead of reaching for the convenience of the modern world, Jinjarli moved to his small kitchen area with deliberate care. He pulled out a piece of lean kangaroo meat and the fresh native greens he had gathered earlier.

He was preparing a simple, nourishing meal. The aroma that soon filled the studio was rich and primal; the earthy scent of meat was a welcome contrast to the chemical tang of the air. As the man worked, using a small pan over a modest gas burner, he leant against the counter and his gaze was fixed on the resolute multimeter. The act of preparing his food and the taste of fire-cooked kangaroo was an anchor to the unbroken songline. It was a physical, culinary connection to the land that mirrored the electrical one he had just measured. Jinjarli chewed slowly, his mind analysing the contrast.

The food provided sustained energy, just as the earth provided sustained flow. He was repairing the sickness of disconnection from the inside out. He realised the 0.03-volt reading wasn't just proof that shoes were a wall; it was confirmation that his ancestors' way of life, eating from the land and touching the land, was the complete protocol for health. The scientific experiment was over, but the living truth had just begun. The multimeter sat on the workbench in Jinjarli's studio, a monument to his crazy idea. He stared at the screen, a small number glowing in the fluorescent light. He hadn't told anyone yet. The rational part of his brain, the part that had listened to Dr Finch, screamed that it was a fluke, a glitch, something that could be dismissed with a single, perfectly logical explanation.

A few weeks later, Jinjarli had not long returned from a walk out of town and he was mixing new paint colours, experimenting with different earthy tones. There was an unexpected knock at the door. His younger cousin, Murray, came bounding in. Murray was a whirlwind of focused energy, eternally attached to his phone. His fingers danced across the screen with an almost alien-like dexterity. He was known around Hammaholl as the one who could fix any tech problem.

"Jinjarli. What's with all the new art?" Murray called out, his eyes already scanning the images on his tablet. He'd been showing Tilly some of his early earthing pieces. "These are… different. Powerful. Like, old stories, but… with wires?" He tilted his head, a keen intelligence in his gaze.

Jinjarli began explaining, the words tumbling out as he articulated the multimeter readings, the sensation by the lake, Uncle Keerray's wisdom and even Dr Finch's dismissal. He described the sickness of disconnection and the ultimate yet simple truth he felt beneath his bare feet. Murray listened, his usual rapid-fire digital chatter replaced by a rare stillness. When Jinjarli finally showed him the multimeter and the 0.03-volt reading, a look of pure shock crossed his face.

"So, you're saying... like, we're batteries and the Earth's a giant charger? And our shoes are, like, insulation?" A wry smile touched his lips, but it wasn't mocking. "That's... wow. That's actually pretty wild."

"It's not just wild, Murray." Jinjarli had a quiet conviction in his voice. "It's ancient and it helps." Murray paused, tapping a thoughtful finger against his chin.

"Okay. So, a tiny voltage. But is it real? Is it consistent? There are so many variables here." He pointed at the multimeter. "One reading is just a story.

We need more." He looked at his cousin, a spark of scientific and cultural curiosity in his eyes.

"Let's go to the source. Let's go to Lake Lumina."

. . . .

The familiar dust of the track near Lake Lumina stained Jinjarli's and Murray's feet as they headed towards the lake. The air hummed with the distant drone of insects, a natural symphony accompanying their crude experiment. The sun was a warm weight on their shoulders, painting the surface of the lake in streaks of gold and bruised purple as it began its slow descent.

"Okay, so the theory is, the more contact, the stronger the connection," Murray said, pulling out his phone to log the data. "Let's try a few different spots and log the data." They started with the drier, sandy patches. Jinjarli pressed the probes against his ankle and into the dry sand. The reading was low, a faint 0.01 volts, barely a flicker.

"Makes sense," Murray muttered, scribbling in his notes. "Not much moisture. It's like a disconnected wire." They moved closer to the water's edge, to a patch of dark, rich mud near the reeds. The mud welcomed Jinjarli's feet. A cool, soft texture that felt alive. He sank the black probe into it, the mud giving way easily. The multimeter, held with a growing confidence, displayed a more significant reading, 0.07 volts. A jolt, far stronger than the first, shot through Jinjarli. He felt the voltage, not just on the screen, but through his body. A resonance that began at his ankle and spread through his whole being. He looked at Murray, who was staring at the numbers with wide-eyed disbelief.

"It's higher," he whispered. "By a factor of seven. It's not a fluke. It's… a pattern."

A battle waged within Jinjarli. The ingrained scepticism of the modern world clashed with the undeniable numbers on the little screen. It really is that simple? A tiny voltage, a connection… is this what Uncle Keerray meant? The readings were small, almost insignificant, yet they resonated with a deep, intuitive knowing. It was no longer just a theory. It was truth. This shared moment solidified their partnership, turning a family conversation into the launch of a scientific quest. The ancient wisdom had been verified by a forgotten modern tool.

Chapter 4

A Bridge of Ochre

The sun had bled out over the horizon line hours before, leaving the vast, ancient chest of the country cooling under a sky incredibly thick with stars. Here, away from the city lights, the Milky Way was not a distant smear but a vibrant river of spirit stretched across the dark. In the centre of the clearing, the fire was already huge. It was built from ironbark and fallen gum. It roared upwards, spitting orange sparks that fought a losing battle against the crushing blackness above. The smell was sharp and intoxicating, burning eucalyptus oil, dry earth and the faint, metallic note of ochre. The mob had gathered slowly; a convergence of families moved in from the shadows. There was a low hum of anticipation, a quiet joy in the greetings.

The elders sat closest to the fire. Their faces were maps of the land itself. As they sat and welcomed everybody, their eyes reflected the flames of the fire. The preparation was finished. The men who would dance stood just beyond the firelight, their chests and thighs painted with intricate patterns of white pipe clay and red ochre, lines and dots that told the stories of each of their specific Dreaming. Their skin belonged to the story as much as the land did.

A silence fell, heavier than the simple absence of noise. It was a deafening silence. A silence that held on. Then. All of a sudden. It began. A single, sharp clack cut the air. Uncle Frank, seated cross-legged, struck the bilma together. The rhythm was steady, a heartbeat accelerated. A second later, the yidaki joined in. Deep and resonant, a vibration that seemed to come from the core of the earth beneath them, not from the long wooden instrument. It was a drone that rattled the ribcages of everyone present, a grounding force that pulled the past into the present. Then the elders began to sing. Their voices were high and nasal. They sang ancient chants in a language that twisted and soared above the drone. It was the songline of this place. It was the acoustic map of the country they stood on.

From the shadows, with a sudden explosion of movement, the dancers emerged. They didn't walk; they stomped. Every footfall was a deliberate hammer blow to the red dust, sending up pungent clouds that turned golden-orange in the firelight. The dust coated their sweating skin, blurring the line between man and earth. The rhythm quickened. The clap-sticks beat faster. The lead dancer, a powerful man in his thirties, broke from the line. His movements shifted. He was no longer just a man; he was the Emu. His head jerked sideways, eyes wide and scanning, his knees bent high and his steps erratic and watchful. The mob watched, mesmerised, as he embodied the ancestor spirit. Behind him, the others moved in unison. They slapped their thighs, the sound like whip cracks over the droning music. Their bodies twisted, vibrating with the energy of the yidaki. The firelight slicked off their sweat, making the white ochre seem to glow from within.

The energy in the clearing grew intense, almost physical. The air was thick with heat and sound. The younger ones in the audience watched with wide eyes, absorbing the lore, feeling the weight of thousands of generations of ceremony pressing down on them. For a long, suspended moment, everything was motion and noise. The singing reached a fever pitch, the stamping feet shook the ground and the fire roared its approval. They were dancing the creation; they were dancing the survival. Then, with a final, thunderous crack of the bilma and a deep, guttural shout from the dancers, it stopped. Instantaneously.

Silence came back into the clearing. The dancers stood frozen for a heartbeat, chests heaving, shrouded in the slowly settling dust. Then the tension broke. A ripple of appreciative murmurs went through the crowd. The lead dancer wiped sweat and dust from his forehead. A tired smile touched his lips as he nodded to his elders. The corroboree was over, but the energy remained. It hung in the smoke and vibrated in the soles of their feet. There was a renewed tether binding the mob to each other and to the grand, starlit country that held them.

. . . .

Firelight danced across the faces of the Gundarra people as they gathered near the main entrance of the community hall, waiting for the beginning of the once-monthly "Community Yarn". The hall was a humble but sturdy building near the west bank of Lake Lumina. Children chased each other across the polished wooden floor. Their laughter was bright against the low hum of conversation. Uncle Keerray sat by the central hearth; his presence was always a grounding force. Jinjarli, who was usually content to blend into the vibrant backdrop, felt a knot of nerves tighten in his stomach. Tonight, he wouldn't just be observing. He had chosen a small and trusted group for his presentation: a few respected aunties, a couple of younger men active in land management and of course, young Tilly. She sat wide-eyed with a mixture of excitement and awe.

Jinjarli had laid out his small collection of artwork – vibrant paintings in ochre and earthy tones, depicting human figures connected by flowing lines to the land. Their bodies radiated health. Besides them lay the multimeter.

"These are beautiful, Jinjarli," Aunty Marra broke the silence; her voice was soft and her fingers were tracing the swirls of red and white pigment on a canvas. "They speak of country, like our old stories."

Jinjarli was blown away.

"Thank you, Aunty. They do. They also speak of something else… something I've been learning about." He picked up the multimeter, its weight becoming familiar now. "Unc, you taught me about the earth's pulse, about how our old people drew strength from the land." Keerray's gaze, ancient and knowing, met his, a silent encouragement. "I found a way to… to show it. With this."

Jinjarli held up the metre. A ripple of murmurs went through the group. The instrument, a piece of the outside world, was foreign here. Jinjarli started by explaining the basics, how the multimeter measured electricity. How the Earth held a subtle charge. He demonstrated with a small piece of basalt from Mount Scoria. He placed one probe on its cool surface and another on his own skin. He showed the flicker of a reading. Then, he put on a thick rubber boot and showed the reading vanish.

"When we wear these," Jinjarli explained, pointing to the pair of boots, "we cut ourselves off from the earth's energy." He spoke of his own fatigue, of Dr Finch's dismissive diagnosis and of how the act of connecting, of earthing, had brought him fleeting moments of clarity.

"I believe," Jinjarli said, his voice gaining quiet conviction, "that this disconnection… it's a disease. Not just for us, but for everyone."

A tense silence fell. Some faces in the firelight showed dawning recognition, a nod to the ancient truths. Young Tilly's eyes gleamed with understanding. But Aunt Tarni, with her back stiff against the wooden bench, spoke; her voice was laced with scepticism.

"This is the white man's tool, Jinjarli. The land doesn't need a machine to tell us its secrets. Our old people knew this. They didn't need numbers." She gestured towards Jinjarli's artwork. "Your paintings, yes. They speak. But this… this science. It cheapens our knowledge. Makes it something they can measure and then… take." The word hung heavy in the air, a potent reminder of two hundred and thirty-five years of dispossession. A few others murmured in agreement, their faces shadowed with caution.

"Auntie Tarni is right," one man said, his eyes on the multimeter. "We fought hard to keep what little we have. If they can measure it, they can control it. This is our spirit, our connection. Not some electric current." Jinjarli felt a pang of frustration. He understood. The fear was real. It's deeply ingrained into the collective memory of the Gundarra people.

"But what if this... this science," Jinjarli emphasised the word, "can be a bridge? A way to show the outside world, in their own language, what we've always known? What if it can help everyone, not just us?"

He looked at Uncle Keerray, whose gaze remained steady, a deep well of support. The debate simmered, a low rumble of conflicting beliefs. The ancient wisdom of his people, a knowledge born of millennia of direct connection, was undeniable. But the methods Jinjarli proposed, the use of a "white man's tool", ignited a deep-seated caution, a historical fear that any new acknowledgement from the dominant culture might come with unforeseen costs. The community, usually so united, was beginning to feel the subtle pull of a divide; a crack was appearing in the very foundation Jinjarli hoped to strengthen. The Gundarra people, who were still wrestling with the implications of Jinjarli's yellow multimeter, focused on the meaning of the tiny electrical reading. The fire crackled, sending sparks up into the night, but the warmth did little to thaw the tension in the room. Auntie Tarni's objection hung heavy in the air, but she wasn't the only one wrestling with the idea.

"It's not just about the white man's numbers, Tarni." Uncle Ray, a man in his fifties who had spent his life working on the council road gangs, spoke up. He leant forward, his elbows resting on his knees, his face illuminated by the firelight. "It's about survival. We've been telling the young ones to get educated, to learn the white man's way so they can get jobs, right? Now Jinjarli uses that education to prove our culture and we growl at him?" He looked around the circle. "I drive the grader all day. My back is broken. If this boy says the earth can fix it and he has a machine that proves it to the boss so I can take my boots off at lunch without getting sacked... then I say let him measure."

"But where does it stop, Ray?" countered a younger woman, Hannah, who worked at the local legal service. She was sharp, protective and cynical. "First they measure the spirit. Then they patent it. Then they sell it back to us. You know how they work. If OmniCorp finds out we have a cure in the dirt, they'll fence it off."

"They can't fence the whole earth, Hannah," Kirri interjected, her phone in her hand but her eyes fierce. "That's the beauty of it. It's too big for them. Jinjarli isn't selling a product. He's giving away the instruction manual. Once the knowledge is out, once it's on the internet, they can't put it back in the box. We aren't losing control; we are taking the lead."

"It is a dangerous path," Old Uncle Sol grunted from the back, tapping his pipe. "Walking between worlds always is. Maybe Ray is right. Maybe we need new weapons for a new fight. The spear didn't stop the gun. Maybe the data stops the bulldozer."

The tension was then broken by a young man, Burra, who voiced the community's central concern, looking from the multimeter to Uncle Keerray.

"Jinjarli, you showed us 0.03 volts. Aunty Marra says your paintings speak of the country's spirit. Is that what the number is, then? Is 0.03 the measurement of the spirit of the land?"

Jinjarli didn't look at the multimeter; he reached instead for the rough, dark chunk of basalt resting next to his artwork. It was another piece he had brought back from a walk up Mount Scoria, whose cool, uneven surface he often traced.

"No. The number is not the spirit. The spirit is what you feel. You remember I told you how touching this basalt gives me a fleeting sense of clarity? How walking barefoot by the lake brought back the quiet strength the town couldn't offer?" He placed the multimeter's probe back on the stone.

"The spirit, the strength of the land, is what heals the static hum. It drains the grey fatigue from the bone.

This little reading, the 0.03 volts, is simply the measurable evidence of that strength. It proves that the feeling is real. It proves that the land has a measurable pulse. The connection is physical, not just faith."

Uncle Keerray nodded slowly, his gaze moving between the ochre paintings and the glowing screen.

"The young fella's machine is just a new type of ear. We have walked this country for sixty-five thousand years. We knew the land had a language. We knew where the cool water was and how the animals moved. The land tells the story. This electricity, this current, it is merely the oldest narrative being told in the newest way." He looked at the community, "We feel the healing. The machine only proves to those who doubt that the wall between your feet and the breathing earth is real. The truth is still the truth; the numbers just make the outside world listen."

The air in the community hall was thick with the debate, the defensive arguments of Aunt Tarni and the analytical counterpoints offered by Jinjarli, focusing heavily on the 0.03-volt reading. Jinjarli, despite his quiet conviction, felt the fatigue of the weeks-long effort settle back into his limbs. He had spent his energy arguing the science and the heavy cloak of weariness was beginning to take over. Young Tilly, however, wasn't listening to the intricate debate about measurability. Her attention was focused on the people and their actions. Her eyes, which had gleamed with understanding during Jinjarli's demonstration, tracked the two central figures: Jinjarli, the young artist, who stood restlessly holding the yellow multimeter, the white man's tool, his shoulders tight with the frustration of having his truth labelled a gimmick and Uncle Keerray. The elder was completely barefoot, his soles touching the earth-built floor, looking utterly anchored and calm, a huge contrast to Jinjarli's visible tension. Tilly's simple observation cut through the intellectual noise of the room. She pointed a small finger towards the elder.

"Uncle Jinjarli, you just proved the earth helps you and you're still standing up there, holding the little yellow box. But Unc there, is sitting on the floor, on the earth and he looks like he's sleeping." The community paused. The young girl's words struck the core of the debate, the disconnect between theory and practice. Jinjarli stared at his own feet. He was so focused on proving the science that he forgot the practice. He was still wearing his rubber boots from the demonstration and he knew his fatigue was visible.

With a silent realisation, Jinjarli gently placed the multimeter down besides the basalt rock. He carefully pulled up the legs of his jeans, took off his boots and sat down on the floor, his bare skin making direct contact with the cool, packed earth near the hearth. He took a deep, shaky breath, allowing the coolness to seep up and settle his tired muscles. The effect was instantaneous and visible. A palpable easing of tension, released from his shoulders. His head, which had felt foggy from weariness, began to clear. This simple, physical act was more persuasive than any number on the screen. The community watched, seeing the difference between Jinjarli the presenter and Jinjarli the patient, finally grounded and restored.

The debate had ended, but the heat of the fire had done nothing to dissipate the cold fear lingering in the air. Jinjarli stood near the cooling hearth. Aunt Tarni's scepticism, that any tool of the outside world would ultimately be used to measure and then... take their spirit, had resonated deeply. The community, usually so united, was now subtly divided. He looked at Uncle Keerray, whose steady gaze still offered only silent support as the sheer weight of the two hundred and thirty-five years of dispossession pressed down on him and the entire gathering. How could Jinjarli argue for the "science" that had once called their healers "witch doctors"? The path he had chosen, the bridge, felt agonisingly thin and solitary in that moment.

Just as the silence threatened to consume his resolve, Jinjarli's younger sister, Kirri, came charging into the mix. She didn't approach the problem with caution or fear; she approached it with the focused fury of a digital native who saw the threat and instantly formulated the counterattack. She swept up the worn boot Jinjarli had used for his demonstration.

"But if it's real, if it can help, why isn't anyone talking about it? Big Pharma won't sell a barefoot cure, will they?" A glint of something sharper, a social justice warrior stirring, entered her gaze. She understood the core conflict immediately: the system profits from the disconnect. She slammed her hand down on the table, ignoring the cooling kangaroo meat and the lingering scent of eucalyptus.

"This isn't just art, Jinjarli. This is a message. A big one and you know what messages need these days?" She didn't wait for an answer. "A platform. A digital drumbeat." She gestured wildly with her phone, her tech-savvy mind buzzing with possibilities. "Your art, your story, those weird little voltage numbers... we need to get this online. Not just your art page. We need videos, explainers, maybe even a little blog. Something that connects the dots for everyone, not just people who spend time barefoot." Her clarity was shocking. She saw the multimeter not as a foreign weapon but as a translation device, a tool to speak the language of numbers to the outside world.

"I can help. I've got the skills. You've got the truth. Let's make some noise." For the first time since this journey began, Jinjarli felt a surge of something other than frustration or cautious hope. He felt a shared purpose. Kirri, with her fast fingers and sharp mind, was the missing piece, the conduit to a wider world that desperately needed to hear the Earth's unbroken song. The fight was no longer an internal, quiet struggle; it was a loud, public crusade and they had just found their megaphone.

....

"This is better than any pill, Unc," Murray murmured, tearing a piece of the tender kangaroo meat. His usual attachment to his phone was gone, replaced by the simple, ancient focus of the feast. Auntie Marra, who had been fiercely supportive during the multimeter demonstration, approached Jinjarli with a warm, gentle smile. Her plate was loaded up with the sweet and charred kangaroo meat and potatoes that were cooked underground.

"Your art speaks of Country, dear. But the food... this is where the healing truly starts. Eating this way, knowing where your strength comes from – that is the ancient wisdom." Jinjarli looked over at Aunt Tarni. The sharp scepticism in her eyes had softened, though hadn't entirely vanished. She was watching the children, the firelight dancing across her face, and eating slowly. The fierce, protective urge in Jinjarli's heart, not just for his own people, but for all of humanity, found peace here. In this shared space of ancestral food and firelight, the sickness of disconnection felt a million miles away. This was the source of strength he was fighting to protect.

Chapter 5

Digital Drumbeats

The following morning, Jinjarli looked rumpled and thoroughly defeated. He stood by the kitchenette in his studio, the air was heavy with the smell of stale coffee and drying paint. He had been painting all night, chasing the fleeting ideas that defied his creative flow, trying to capture the feeling of the voltage on canvas and achieving only muddy swirls of frustration. Now, a thick weariness had settled over him. The heavy sluggishness was palpable. He held a fresh mug, barely having started his fourth coffee. His limbs mirrored the dull, lifeless state of the colours on the canvases leaning against the wall.

A sudden, sharp knock at the glass door snapped him back into the present. Before he could even shuffle forward to unlock it, the door slid open with a loud bang and Kirri came bursting in. She was a whirlwind of focused energy that immediately clashed with the studio's exhausted atmosphere. Her jacket was zipped tight, her shoes were laced for action and her fingers, already dancing on her phone screen. She was primed for war.

"You look cooked, mate," Kirri said, surveying the scene, the overturned paint rag, the half-empty coffee mugs and the exhaustion that clung to his limbs like wet wool.

"Were you up chasing ghosts again? Didn't get much rest, eh?" Jinjarli rubbed his eyes, the movement heavy and reluctant.

"Don't, Kirri. I was trying to work. My head's like mud. I was seriously thinking about just pulling the blinds and calling it a day." Kirri ignored his plea. She strode directly to his workbench, placing her phone down with a decisive tap next to the multimeter and the basalt chunk.

"Forget the paint for a bit. We're not doing art today; we're doing warfare," she stated, her voice calm and firm, brimming with a no-nonsense energy. "You proved it. You got the 0.07 volts at the lake. We've got the story of the sickness of disconnection and the cure that Dr Finch missed. So, is this where I'll set the laptop up?" She didn't wait for an answer. She began clearing a space on his sacred workbench, sweeping aside his brushes and jars of pigment with alarming efficiency.

"Hey, watch it." Jinjarli snapped, stepping forward to protect his space. "That's pure ochre from the riverbed. Don't just shove it aside."

"It's dirt, Jinjarli," Kirri said, pulling a sleek, silver laptop from her bag. "Valuable dirt, I know, but right now, bandwidth is more important than pigment." She started pulling cables out of her bag: white ones, black ones and braided ones. They looked like snakes coiling over his workbench.

"Do you have to put the modem there?" Jinjarli asked, wincing as she placed a blinking black box right next to his basalt rock. "That rock is… It's a grounding point. It's quiet energy. That modem is just… noise." Kirri looked at him, holding a power cable in mid-air.

"That modem is the only way your quiet energy gets out of this shed, Bro. You want the world to know? Then we need the noise." She plugged it in. The lights on the modem blinked rapidly, green, orange, green. It felt aggressive against the stillness of the stone. "And this," she said, holding up a tangle of charging cords. "I need a power board. Where is it?"

"Under the easel," Jinjarli grumbled. "But it's for the lamp."

"Not anymore." She dived under the easel, wrestling with the dust bunnies and emerged triumphant. She plugged everything in. The workbench, usually a place of organic chaos, was now a spiderweb of silicon and copper. Jinjarli leant against the wall, sipping his coffee, watching his sister colonise his sanctuary.

"You're ruining the Feng shui, Kirri."

"I'm optimising the workflow," she shot back, cracking her knuckles. "You've got the truth, Jinjarli. But the truth is useless if it's whispering in a shed. I'm giving it a microphone."

The moment Kirri made her decision to help, the studio stopped being just an art space and became a mission control centre. She immediately designated the corner near the back window as her domain, creating a sharp, functional contrast to Jinjarli's creative chaos. Kirri's workspace was defined by speed and efficiency. She didn't use turpentine or ochre; she used fibre optics and code. She pulled out a portable ring light that cast a harsh, circular halo on the ceiling and a high-speed mobile hotspot that hummed softly. The sleek, pale metal of her gear lay right next to Jinjarli's rough basalt rock and the yellow multimeter, a perfect symbol of their necessary, even though clashing, alliance.

While Jinjarli was wrestling with the lingering fatigue and the strong, heavy reluctance to start painting, Kirri was a whirlwind of activity.

"Right, Unbroken Songlines. Clean domain. SEO optimised for earthing and natural health Australia. Link the YouTube channel for the video proofs." She worked at a frantic, exhilarating pace. She took the raw footage they had shot on Murray's phone – Jinjarli's quiet conviction, his ochre-stained hands holding the probes and the stark jump of the numbers from zero to 0.07V – and began to slice and dice it.

"Jinjarli, look at this visual hook," she called out, spinning her laptop around. On the screen, she had created a split-screen edit. On the left, Jinjarli is standing on the rubber mat, looking tired, the meter reading 0.00v. On the right, the moment his feet hit the mud, the meter spiked to 0.07v and there was a visible relaxation in his shoulders.

"I overlaid a graphic of electron flow," she explained, pointing to little animated blue dots rushing from the ground into the video – Jinjarli's feet. "It makes the invisible visible. It's like a magic trick, but it's physics." Jinjarli, sipping his lukewarm coffee, stared at the screen. The blue dots made it look like a science fiction movie.

"It's not a trick, Kirri. It's the truth."

"Exactly. And we're selling the truth." Kirri countered. "But people have an attention span of three seconds. You have to hook 'em. She hit Publish. The room went quiet. Just the buzz of the fridge and the distant sound of a magpie.

"Now what?" Jinjarli asked.

"Now," Kirri said, leaning back and crossing her arms behind her head, "we wait for the algorithm to wake up." It didn't take long. Ten minutes later, Kirri's phone pinged. A single, lonely sound.

"First view," she announced. "Probably Mum." Then another ping. Then two in rapid succession. Kirri sat up, her eyes glued to the analytics dashboard.

"Okay, Murray just shared it to the local footy group page. That's fifty eyeballs." She refreshed the page. The view count jumped from 12 to 87.

"Read them," Jinjarli said, moving closer. "What are they saying?" Kirri scrolled down. "The first comment is from... 'FootyLegend99'," he says, "Is this why I play better when it rains? Mud power?" Jinjarli smiled.

"He's joking, but... he's actually right. Wet grass is more conductive." Kirri refreshed again. 150 views.

"Okay, here we go," she muttered. "The shares are starting."

"User 'EarthMother_Vic' says, 'I have felt this for years, but my husband calls me crazy. Thank you for showing the numbers. I am crying watching this." Jinjarli felt a lump in his throat. That was it. That was the connection.

"Here's another one," Kirri read, her voice softening. "User TiredTom: I work in a warehouse on concrete floors for 10 hours a day. By Friday I want to cut my legs off. I'm going to take my boots off at lunch today. Worth a try."

"Tell him to find grass," Jinjarli said urgently. "Concrete won't work if it's dry."

"I'm replying now," Kirri typed furiously. "Hey Tom, find damp grass or dirt. Concrete is insulated if it's sealed." With the light comes the shadow. As the view count ticked past 500, the tone began to shift.

"Ah, here come the cookers," Kirri muttered, her brow furrowing. "User RationalMan_45: This is complete rubbish. Pseudo-science for hippies who can't afford shoes. Go get a job." Jinjarli flinched. The hostility was sudden and sharp.

"And another one," Kirri read, scanning quickly. "User Medi-Watch: Dangerous advice. You'll get hookworm or tetanus. Trust doctors, not artists playing with electricians' tools."

"They're missing the point," Jinjarli said, frustration rising. "It's not about being anti-doctor. It's about…"

"It doesn't matter, Bro," Kirri interrupted, her eyes gleaming. "Look at the engagement stats. Every time someone comments to call you an idiot, the algorithm pushes the video to ten more people who might agree with you. Controversy is fuel." She spun the phone around again. "We're trending locally. Look at the comments. "I thought I was the only one feeling this disconnected. That's us, Jinjarli. We hit a nerve."

"Look. An email from a health forum in Japan. They've translated the piece. They're saying your sickness of disconnection resonates globally. We're not just local anymore, Bro. We're international." Jinjarli, rubbing the tiredness from his eyes, felt the fatigue competing with a rising, overwhelming sense of awe. He was ready for bed, but his story was now a global wildfire and his sister was the master of the flame. The digital drumbeat had begun and it was very, very loud.

"We need more content," Kirri announced an hour later. "The people are asking how it works. We need an explainer video. A 'How-To'." She had designated a small, bare wall as the backdrop for filming Jinjarli's scientific explainers. She had spent thirty minutes setting up the ring light and securing the multimeter leads for a perfect close-up shot.

"...and here, Jinjarli demonstrates how the rubber sole acts as a perfect insulator, creating the wall between your feet and the breathing earth." Jinjarli was wearing his only clean shirt, holding the multimeter like a holy relic. He felt ridiculous, posing for a phone camera while Kirri shouted directions like a Hollywood director.

"And this, as Uncle Keerray taught, is why we experience the sickness of disconnection."

"Cut." Kirri yelled. "More energy, Jinjarli. You sound like you're reading a eulogy. Sell it."

"I'm not selling anything, Kirri. I'm telling."

"Same thing. Go again. Action." Just as Kirri zoomed in for a tight shot of the 0.03-volt reading, Jinjarli shifted his weight. His foot, still slightly damp from the morning walk and coated in the fine red dust of the studio floor, dragged across the pristine white backdrop paper she had laid down. He left a distinct, bright red ochre footprint right across the designated filming zone. Kirri dropped her phone. She was horrified.

"Jinjarli! You walked right through the colour palette. We can't film here now. That's going to look like a CSI forensic scene." Jinjarli looked down at the footprint. It was perfect. The arch, the toes, the heel. A stamp of red earth on the sterile white paper.

"What? It's just earth," he said, shrugging. "It's the most natural thing here. It's a spontaneous land-art testimonial. See? The ochre is part of the earth's memory. It remembers where we walked." Kirri sighed, pinching the bridge of her nose.

"No, Bro. On camera, it's just "dirt". It looks messy. And it just ruined my white balance. Go stand next to the basalt until the floor dries and for the love of the ancestors, wipe your feet."

The sun was setting and Jinjarli, exhausted by the afternoon's digital performance, was finally attempting a period of quiet reflection. He had found a corner away from the buzzing electronics, sitting cross-legged next to his basalt rock, hoping to absorb some of its cool, quiet strength. He closed his eyes, focusing on his breathing, trying to find the quiet hum he felt by the lake. Suddenly, Kirri's voice boomed from the digital hub; she was on a video conference with Murray and was using her loudspeaker.

"Murray, listen. We need to pivot. The comments are asking about electromagnetic interference. We need a clean IP address log from the northern suburbs to counteract the Big Pharma push."

"...Yeah, I'm tracing the subnet now. But tell Unc to stop sending me art photos. My hard drive is full of ochre." Murray's voice crackled from the laptop. It was tinny and distorted. Jinjarli opened one eye and whispered.

"Kirri. I'm trying to ground. I can't find the Earth's pulse when you're discussing IP addresses at maximum volume." Kirri shrugged and covered the laptop mic with her hand.

"Just use the basalt, mate. Multitask. You're lucky I'm here. If it wasn't for this noise, Dr Finch would have already filed your truth under 'F' for folklore." She uncovered the mic. "Go ahead, Murray. I'm listening." Jinjarli closed his eyes again, shaking his head. He realised this was the new reality. The silence of the Songline was now going to be defended by the loudest noise imaginable. And as much as he hated the cable snakes on his bench, he knew his sister was right. Without the noise, the silence would never be heard.

Chapter 6

The Belly Of The Beast

The late afternoon air outside the Hammaholl Town Hall was usually a quiet affair, disturbed only by the occasional passing ute or the distant bark of a dog. Today, however, the atmosphere was charged with a sharp, frantic energy that tasted of ozone mixed with confrontation. Jinjarli stepped out of Murray's car and immediately felt the change in his senses. The setting sun cast long, hard shadows across the pavement and the chaotic noise was unsettling. A crowd had gathered at the base of the municipal steps. It wasn't the natural gathering of a community meeting. It was a staged event. On the left stood the Gundarra people and their local supporters. They were a sea of quiet resolve, dressed in earth tones. They stood in loose, comfortable clusters. They held no signs. Their presence was their protest. Uncle Keerray stood at the front, leaning on his walking stick. On the right, separated by a thin line of nervous-looking police officers, was a very different group. They held professionally printed placards, glossy and uniform, bearing slogans like Public Safety First and Science Saves Lives. The logo of The Busguardian Group, a local community action organisation that Kirri had traced back to pharmaceutical funding, was discreetly printed in the corner of every sign.

"They look like they're auditioning for a commercial," Murray muttered, adjusting the focus on his camera rig. "Look at them. Same haircuts, same angry-but-concerned expressions. They're paid actors, Cuz."

"Let them act," Uncle Keerray said, his voice a low rumble that seemed to travel under the chanting. "The noise is only loud because they are afraid the silence is starting to be heard." As Jinjarli walked towards the steps, the chanting from the Busguardian side surged.

"Real Cures. Real Doctors. Real Science." It was a rhythmic, mechanical sound, devoid of any real passion but full of manufactured outrage. Jinjarli felt the pavement hard and unforgiving beneath his bare feet, a deliberate choice he had made that morning. The synthetic coldness of the concrete that stung his skin was a physical reminder of the hostile ground he was about to enter. He reached the heavy glass doors of the Town Hall. They hissed open automatically, exhaling a gust of conditioned air that hit Jinjarli like a physical blow. If the outside was hostile, the inside was suffocating. The transition was immediate and jarring. The air in the foyer didn't smell like air; it smelled of industrial-strength Lemon-Fresh floor cleaner and the metallic tang of an overworked aircon unit. It was the scent of sterility, of a place where bacteria, dirt and life itself were scrubbed away.

Jinjarli stepped into the foyer. The building instantly attacked him. It wasn't just the temperature, though the air conditioning was set to a bone-dry eighteen degrees, that sucked the moisture right out of his eyes. It was the sound. To anyone wearing shoes, the room was silent. To Jinjarli, barefoot and open, the room was screaming. He could feel the hum of the fluorescent tubes overhead, a high-frequency mosquito whine that drilled into the base of his skull. It was the sound of excited argon gas trapped in glass. It vibrated with an anger that had nowhere to go. He took a step onto the industrial carpet. A spark of static electricity bit his big toe. The floor was a battery of friction. Every synthetic fibre in the weave was rubbing against the next, building up a charge that coated his skin in an invisible, prickly film. Even the air tasted metallic, like licking a 9-volt battery. It smelled of burnt toner dust and the ammonia-sharp burn of industrial floor polish.

Jinjarli looked at the receptionist behind the Plexiglas shield. She was typing. Her fingers clicking away on the plastic keys. Her eyes were glazed by the blue light of the monitor. She looked like a specimen in a jar. Jinjarli felt the muscles in his neck tighten, a physical reaction to the electromagnetic soup he was wading through. He craved the mud. He craved the silence of the wet earth that absorbed noise instead of amplifying it. Here, in the heart of the town, he was standing inside a machine that was trying to grind him down to dust. The low-frequency hum of the fluorescent lights overhead drilled into his skull, a relentless buzz that sat just on the edge of his hearing. He rubbed his arms. The hair stood on end, not from cold but from the sheer electrical tension of the room. It was the perfect antithesis to the lake. It was a box designed to disconnect.

"Breathe," Kirri whispered besides him, seeing his jaw tighten. "You're walking into the belly of the beast. Don't let them eat you."

. . . .

The main chamber was packed. The room was divided down the middle, a physical manifestation of the town's fracture. Brendan O'Malley, the owner of the local hardware store, sat in the fifth row, right on the aisle. He was a man who prided himself on his common sense. He'd known Jinjarli's family for years. He had bought art from him once for his wife's birthday. He liked the kid. He also looked up at the stage where Dr Alistair Finch was taking his seat. Finch had set Brendan's leg when he broke it playing footy twenty years ago. Finch was the reason his father's heart was still ticking. Brendan shifted in his plastic chair, feeling torn. He watched Jinjarli walk to the podium, barefoot, looking dusty and a bit wild. Then he looked at Finch, immaculate in his charcoal suit, his silver hair perfectly coiffed, radiating an aura of calm, expensive competence.

The kid's got heart, Brendan thought, rubbing his chin. But Finch has got the medicine. You don't fix a leaking pipe with a song, do you? You fix it with a wrench. He looked around at the protesters in the back, then at the elders in the front. He felt like the town was holding its breath, waiting to see if it would exhale logic or magic. The moderator, a councilman named Gary who looked like he'd rather be anywhere else, suddenly tapped the microphone. The feedback squeal made everyone wince.

"We will begin with Mr Jinjarli," Gary mumbled. Jinjarli stood. He gripped the sides of the podium. He spoke of the weariness. He spoke of the 0.03 volts. He spoke of the insulating silence. He described the rubber barrier that turned men into batteries with nowhere to discharge. He spoke with passion. His voice trembled slightly with the raw honesty of his experience. He projected the image of his art, the human figure glowing with earth energy. When he finished, there was scattered applause, passionate from his side and polite but hesitant from the middle. Then, Dr Finch stood up. He didn't rush. He buttoned his jacket with a slow, deliberate movement that commanded total attention. He walked to the microphone, not like a man entering a fight, but like a professor entering a lecture hall to correct a promising but confused student.

"Thank you, Councilman," Finch began. His voice was a rich, polished baritone that seemed to warm the sterile room. He turned to Jinjarli and offered a small, sad smile.

"And thank you, Jinjarli. I must say, your presentation was... moving. Truly. The poetry of your culture, the imagery of the land... it is a beautiful thing. We all feel the stress of the modern world, don't we?" He looked out at the audience, making eye contact with Brendan in the fifth row. "We all feel that heaviness. We all yearn for a simpler time." He paused, letting the empathy hang in the air. He was validating the feeling, disarming the anger.

"But", Finch continued, his voice hardening just a fraction. He sounded like steel wrapped in velvet. "We are not here to discuss poetry. We are here to discuss public health and public health is not built on feelings. It is not built on "vibes" or "currents" that only the chosen few can feel." He paced slowly across the stage. "Medicine is a discipline of measurement. Of proof. When your child has a fever, do you want a story about the wind? Or do you want antibiotics that have been tested in trials and are proven to work? When a heart stops, we don't restart it with bare feet in the mud. We use precision. We use science." He turned back to Jinjarli, his expression almost pitying. "To suggest that the complex, biological reality of human disease can be cured by simply taking off one's shoes... it is not just unscientific, it is dangerous. It offers false hope to the suffering." Finch lowered his voice to a grave whisper, "It is the cruellest thing you can give a patient. Let us not romanticise the mud," Finch said, his voice dropping to a hush that silenced the room. "Nature is not a benevolent mother. She is an indifferent force. We built cities to escape the cold. We paved roads to rise above the filth. We invented shoes not to sever our connection but to protect our soles from the cut and the infection. We created this 'sterile' world because the natural world was short, brutal and full of pain. To go back to the dirt is not healing; it is regression. It is tearing down the fortress we built to keep you safe."

Brendan, in the fifth row, felt himself nodding. He's right, Brendan thought. It's nice to think the earth loves us, but when the chips are down, I want the antibiotics. Finch sat down. The room erupted in applause, louder and more confident than Jinjarli's. The logic was seductive. It felt safe. Jinjarli stood there, feeling the weight of the room shifting away from him. Finch had used words to build a fortress of logic that Jinjarli's poetry couldn't penetrate. He looked at the multimeter on the table. It looked like a cheap toy next to Finch's authority. He needed to break the fortress.

"Dr Finch talks about false hope," Jinjarli spoke, leaning into the mic. His voice was quieter now, forcing the room to lean in. "He talks about measurement." Jinjarli reached down and picked up the multimeter. He held it up. It was a block of yellow plastic, ugly and utilitarian.

"This is not poetry," Jinjarli said. "This is a tool. The same tool an electrician uses to wire your house. The same tool you trust to keep your lights on." He picked up the chunk of basalt rock he had brought from Mount Scoria. He placed it on the podium with a heavy thud.

"Dr Finch says we cannot measure the connection. He says it is a story." Jinjarli turned the dial on the meter. The click echoed in the silence. He held up the black probe.

"This is the earth." He pressed it to the stone. He held up the red probe.

"This is me." He pressed it to his wrist. He turned the screen towards the audience. The numbers danced for a second, then settled. 0.05 V.

"That is not a story," Jinjarli said, his voice ringing out. "That is a circuit. That is current flowing from the stone into my blood. You say you want measurement, Doctor? Here is your measurement. You say you want proof? Here is the voltage." He looked directly at Brendan in the fifth row.

"You don't need to believe in magic, mate. You just need to believe in electricity." The hush that fell over the room was absolute. It wasn't the silence of respect; it was the silence of a paradigm shift. The visual evidence, the cold, hard number on the screen, had punctured the velvet balloon of Finch's rhetoric. Even Finch stared at the screen, his perfectly sculpted eyebrow twitching just once.

The adrenaline didn't crash until they were well away from the Town Hall. They had piled into Murray's ute: Jinjarli, Kirri, Murray and Uncle Keerray. The drive out of town was silent. The streetlights flickered past, rhythmic bursts of orange light illuminating their tired faces. Jinjarli's hands were shaking. He gripped his knees, trying to stop the tremors. The confrontation had taken everything out of him; he felt hollowed out, scraped clean by the stress. The silence in the ute was heavy, not peaceful. It was the ringing silence that follows an explosion. Murray gripped the steering wheel, his knuckles white, navigating the vehicle out of the town centre. As the streetlights of Hammaholl thinned out, replaced by the encroaching dark of the highway, a low-fuel light pinged on the dashboard.

"Need juice," Murray muttered, flicking the indicator. He pulled into a brightly lit 'Servo' on the edge of town. It was a beacon of artificiality in the night, a canopy of blinding white LEDs hovering over pumps of concrete and steel.

Jinjarli opened the passenger door and stepped out. The sensation was immediate and violent. The forecourt wasn't just hard; it was vibrating. The concrete was soaked in decades of spilt diesel and oil, a chemical layer that seemed to sear against the soles of his bare feet. The air here didn't move; it hung suspended, thick with the fumes of petroleum and the hot exhaust of a semi-trailer idling nearby.

"I'll get it," Jinjarli said, his voice sounding thin to his own ears. He needed to move, to shake off the static of the Town Hall, but this place was just a concentrated dose of the same poison. He walked towards the sliding glass doors, the automatic mechanism hissing open to welcome him into the refrigerated interior.

Inside, the assault on his senses was total. The air conditioning was set to a bone-chilling temperature, drying the sweat on his skin instantly. The hum of the refrigeration units lining the walls was a physical pressure, a constant, aggressive drone that drilled into his temples. He walked down the aisle to pay, past rows of colourful, plastic-wrapped lollies, energy drinks and chips. Everything was sealed. Everything was preserved. Everything was dead.

"Pump four, thanks," Jinjarli said to the attendant, a young man with dark circles under his eyes, illuminated by the blue light of the register screen. The kid looked at Jinjarli, his gaze drifting down to his bare, dusty feet on the Lino, then back up. There was no judgement, just a dull, glazed exhaustion.

"Thirty-eight dollars," the kid mumbled, scanning a can of Red Bull for himself. "You want a receipt?" Jinjarli looked at the kid, really looked at him. He saw the grey tint to his skin, the slight tremor in his hand as he reached for the energy drink. The kid was standing on a rubber mat, behind a counter, under fluorescent lights, surrounded by sugar and caffeine, trying to buy enough artificial energy to get through a shift that was draining his life force.

"No receipt," Jinjarli whispered. He wanted to reach out, to tell the kid to take his shoes off and to go stand on the patch of dead grass behind the air pump outside. You're just a battery running dry, he thought. This whole place is designed to drain you.

He walked back out to the ute, the contrast between the refrigerated air and the night air hitting him like a sucker punch. He climbed into the passenger seat and slammed the door, curling his toes, trying to retract them from the memory of the oily concrete.

"Let's go, Murray," he said, his teeth chattering slightly. "Get me away from the lights. I can feel them buzzing in my teeth." Murray glanced at him, seeing the tremor in his hands.

"We're going to the fire, Cuz. We're going to the dirt. Just hold on." The four of them drove on, again in silence, until they were past the lights, past the fumes and back in the country.

"Pull over," Elder Keerray said softly. Murray steered the ute off the road, down a dirt track that led toward the back of Keerray's property. They got out. The air here was different. The smell of exhaust and floor cleaner was gone, replaced by the sharp, clean scent of eucalyptus and cooling dust. Keerray had a small fire pit near the creek bed. Within minutes, Murray had a fire crackling. The flames licked at the darkness, pushing it back. Jinjarli sat on a log, staring into the coals. He felt like he was vibrating, the echo of the town hall's static still buzzing in his teeth.

"You did good, boy," Keerray said, handing him a tin mug of tea. "You held your ground."

"Did I?" Jinjarli asked, his voice cracking. "Finch... he's so smooth. He made me feel like a child with a toy. Did you see the shopkeeper? Brendan? He was nodding along with him."

"He was nodding because he was scared," Keerray said, poking the fire with a stick. "Finch offers them safety. You offer them the unknown. People always choose safety first."

"But the metre..." Kirri said, sitting cross-legged on the dirt. "The look on their faces when the numbers came up. You broke the spell, Jinjarli. You saw it. Finch blinked." Jinjarli took a sip of the tea. It was hot and sweet. He took a deep breath, letting the smoke of the fire fill his lungs. He could feel the ground beneath his feet, real ground, not carpet. The vibration in his body began to slow down, matching the rhythm of the fire.

"It's not over," Jinjarli whispered. "That was just the first round. Finch isn't going to stop. He looked... offended. Like I insulted his god."

"You did," Murray chuckled darkly. "His god is control and you just showed everyone that the biggest power source in the world is wild, free and right under their feet." Elder Keerray looked up at the stars, which were bright and hard above the tree line.

"Rest now. Let the fire burn the town out of you. Tomorrow, the shadow will be longer. But tonight... tonight, the songline was heard." Jinjarli closed his eyes. The static faded. The hum of the aircon was replaced by the chirp of crickets. He was back on Country and he knew, with a certainty that settled deep in his gut, that he had started a war he couldn't walk away from.

Chapter 7

The Squatter's Legacy

The offices of Mick Davies were located in a squat, brick building that seemed designed to repel sunlight. To Jinjarli, stepping through the heavy glass doors felt like walking into a tomb. The air inside didn't flow; it was heavily recycled and pushed through dusty vents with a low, aggressive drone that vibrated in his teeth. It smelled of scorched coffee, printer toner and the stale, nervous sweat of deadlines. Jinjarli stood in the entrance, his bare feet shifting on the thin, industrial-grade carpet. He could feel the static electricity building up instantly, a prickly, uncomfortable heat rising up his shins. It was the physical manifestation of the wall Uncle Keerray spoke of. A building designed to insulate its occupants from the earth and trap them in a loop of artificial energy. He felt a familiar fog begin to descend on his mind, the sharp clarity of the morning dissolving into the murky sluggishness of the indoors.

Mick Davies sat at a desk that looked like a paper explosion. He was a man who wore his cynicism like a comfortable old coat. He was typing furiously, a cigarette unlit and forgotten in the corner of his mouth. His face was illuminated by the harsh glare of two computer monitors.

"Take a seat, Jinjarli. Just move the… piles," Mick grunted, not looking up. Jinjarli carefully moved a stack of council meeting minutes and sat on a plastic chair. It squeaked, a sharp, synthetic sound that cut through the room's drone. Mick finally stopped typing. He spun his chair around, looking at Jinjarli over the top of his reading glasses. He looked tired. Not the good, physical tiredness of a day's work on the land, but the deep, grey exhaustion of a man who spent his life chasing shadows.

"Right," Mick said, leaning back and crossing his arms. "Let's cut the fluff. I saw the forum. I saw Dr Finch dress you down. I saw you hold up a rock like it was an iPhone." He picked up a pen and clicked it rhythmically. "I'm a journalist, Jinjarli. I deal in facts. Documents. Paper trails. What you're selling… this earth energy… to be honest, mate, it sounds like magic crystals. It sounds like something you buy at a weekend market to feel better about your divorce." Jinjarli didn't flinch. He expected this.

"It's not magic, Mick. It's physics. You just don't have the tools to measure it yet."

"Dr Finch has the tools," Mick countered, his voice sharp. "He has the degrees. He says you are dreaming."

"Finch lives in a box," Jinjarli said, gesturing around the room. "Like this one. Can't you feel it, Mick?"

"Feel what? The deadline looming?"

"The hum," Jinjarli said softly. "The vibration of this room. The lights are buzzing. The computer fans are spinning. The static in the carpet. It's a noise, Mick. A constant, screaming noise that your body is fighting every second. You're so used to it that you don't hear it anymore. But your body does. That's why your shoulders are up by your ears. That's why you look like you haven't had a real night's sleep in years." Mick stopped clicking the pen. He frowned, his hand instinctively going to his stiff neck.

"You're telling me my carpet is making me tired?"

"I'm telling you that you are an electrical being living in a rubber cage," Jinjarli said. "When I walk on the land, the noise stops. The mud, the stone… it drains the static. It quiets the scream. That's the language of the bone Uncle Keerray talks about. It's not magic. It's just… plugging back in." Mick stared at him for a long moment. He looked at the unlit cigarette, then at the piles of paper, then back at Jinjarli's bare feet on the carpet. The cynicism was still there, but a crack had appeared.

"Okay," Mick sighed, tossing the pen onto the desk. "I don't know about the physics. That's above my pay grade. But I know people. And I know when someone is selling snake oil and I know when someone believes what they're saying." He leant forward. "You believe it. And Finch… Finch was too defensive. A doctor confident in his science doesn't get that angry about a rock." Mick pulled a fresh notepad towards him. "I can't write a story about vibes, Jinjarli. I need something hard. If this earthing works and it's free… why is Finch so scared of it?"

"Because you can't patent the ground," Kirri said.

She had been standing quietly by the door, observing. Now she stepped forward, dropping a heavy laptop bag onto Mick's desk. She unzipped it, revealing her setup.

"Jinjarli handles the spirit. I handle the system. You want a story, Mick? Let's follow the money." The investigation began not with a sprint, but with a grind.

Kirri transformed a corner of Mick's cluttered office into a digital command centre. She bridged the gap between Mick's old-school investigative instincts, the phone calls, paper archives and public records requests with her own high-speed data mining. For three hours, the room was a symphony of frustration.

"Dead end," Mick muttered, slamming down the phone. "The Regional Health Board minutes are redacted." Commercial in confidence. "Since when is public health commercial?"

"I'm hitting walls too," Kirri said, her fingers flying across her keyboard. "Finch's directorships are clean. He's on the board of the hospital, a local charity and the golf club. Boring. Squeaky clean."

"There has to be a link," Mick said, pacing the small room. The air was getting stale, thick with smoke from the cigarette he'd finally lit. "He's not just protecting his ego. He's protecting a fortress. The way he spoke at the forum… We prefer compounds we can measure. He sounded like a brochure. " Jinjarli watched them from the corner. He felt useless in this digital hunt, but he held the space. He kept one hand on his basalt rock, anchoring the room, keeping the noise manageable so they could work.

"Check the spouses," Mick suggested, rubbing his temples. "Check the silent partners."

"Already running it," Kirri said, her eyes scanning streams of data. "Nothing on Hazel Finch. She's a librarian. Wait." She paused. "There's a pattern in the board members. Look at this." Mick leant over her shoulder. Jinjarli stood up and moved closer.

"This is a network graph of the Regional Health Advisory Committee," Kirri explained, pointing to a spiderweb of dots on her screen. "Here's Finch. Here's Dr Vance from the NHOA. Here's a guy named Marcus Howell."

"Who's Howell?" Mick asked.

"He's a consultant," Kirri said, typing the name into a search bar. "But look at his history. He sits on the board of the Horizon Investment Group."

"Horizon," Mick mused. "They're the ones developing the new medical centre in Hammaholl. Real estate developers."

"Are they?" Kirri clicked a few more keys. "Let's look at Horizon's portfolio." The screen refreshed. A list of subsidiaries scrolled past. Construction firms. Logistics. Then, buried in the diversified assets fund: VitaGlobal Holdings.

"VitaGlobal," Mick whispered. "They manufacture anti-anxiety meds and painkillers. Keep digging," Mick ordered, his voice tight. "That's two degrees of separation. We need a direct line." Kirri bit her lip.

"Horizon is a private equity firm. They don't have to disclose their individual shareholders."

"They do if they tender for government contracts," Mick said, a shark-like grin appearing. "Did Horizon bid for the hospital expansion?"

"Checking… Yes. 2023."

"Pull the tender document. Section 4. Beneficial Ownership." Kirri navigated through the government archive. The file was huge, a PDF scanned from a paper copy. She scrolled down, past the legalese, past the architectural drawings, to the fine print at the back. The room went silent.

"There," Mick breathed, pointing a nicotine-stained finger at the screen. It wasn't a smoking gun; it was a cannon. Listed under the Beneficial Ownership Trust for Horizon Investment Group were a series of family trusts. There, nestled among the obscure corporate entities, was The Redboulder Family Trust. Mick let out a low whistle.

"Redboulder."

"What is it?" Kirri asked. "Sounds like a quarry."

"It's bigger than a quarry," Mick said, leaning back, his eyes hard. "Redboulder is the name of the massive pastoral station north of Hammaholl. It's old money, Kirri. We're talking landed gentry. Wool barons from the 1800s." He tapped the screen. "I always thought Finch was just a doctor who married well. But this… this means he comes from the kind of family that has owned half the district for a century. They don't just invest in land; they are the land lords." She opened a new tab and searched the business registry for the trust.

Trustee: Alistair James Finch.

"Gotcha," Mick exhaled, the sound loud in the quiet room.

"He's not just a doctor protecting his ego," Mick said, pacing again, energy surging through him. "He's a squatter. He's the heir to Redboulder Station. He has a direct financial interest in keeping things exactly the way they are because his family has been profiting off this land and the people on it since settlement." Mick stopped pacing and looked at Jinjarli, his eyes hard and bright.

"He's not fighting you because you're wrong, mate. He's fighting you because you're reclaiming the dirt he thinks he owns."

"And it gets worse," Kirri said. She had kept digging while Mick paced. "Look at the NHOA board members. Dr Vance? Her husband is the Chief Legal Officer for OmniCorp. The guy sitting next to her? Former VP of Sales for VitaGlobal."

She spun the laptop around so they could see the full picture. It was a diagram of corruption, intricate and terrifying.

"It's a web," Kirri said, her voice trembling slightly. "It's not just Finch. It's the whole structure. The people regulating the medicine, the people prescribing the medicine and the people selling the medicine… they're all in the same bed. Literally and financially." Mick stared at the screen, smoke curling from his lips.

"Regulatory capture," he said, "the NHOA isn't protecting the public. It's protecting the patent. If Jinjarli's free cure gains traction, VitaGlobal's stock drops. Horizon's portfolio takes a hit. Finch's retirement fund shrinks." Jinjarli looked at the names on the screen. They were just words, glowing pixels on a glass screen, but they represented a wall higher than any physical barrier.

"They aren't fighting my science," he realised, a cold clarity washing over him. "They are fighting for their money."

"Exactly," Mick said, grabbing his jacket off the back of his chair. He reached for his pack of cigarettes, a shark-like grin splitting his tired face. For the first time in weeks, the oppressive, recycled hum of the office felt like a triumphant buzz. They had the smoking gun. They had the map of the enemy's fortress. "And that, my friends, is a front-page story."

The room fell into a brief, heavy silence of shared victory. The click of Kirri's keyboard stopped. The hum of the computer fans seemed to recede. They were three people in a small room who had just uncovered a giant. The sound of the phone ringing shattered the moment like a hammer through glass. It wasn't the soft, digital trill of a mobile; it was the harsh, mechanical rattle of the old office landline that sat on the corner of Mick's desk like a dusty relic. It rang with a violent, brassy urgency that made Kirri jump in her seat. Mick froze, his hand halfway to his pocket. He stared at the phone. Nobody called the landline anymore. Not advertisers. Not sources. Only people who wanted to make sure you were exactly where they thought you were. The sound of the phones ring echoed off the cheap walls, insistent and angry. The grin vanished from Mick's face, replaced by a grey, focused tension. He picked it up slowly.

"Davies." Jinjarli watched Mick's face transform. It went blank, then hard. The flush of victory drained from his cheeks, leaving him looking sallow under the fluorescent lights. The air in the room shifted instantly from the heat of the chase to the cold chill of exposure.

"I see," Mick said. His voice was dangerously calm, but his knuckles were white on the receiver. "Is that a threat, Barry?" He listened for another moment, his eyes flicking to the diagram on

Kirri's screen. "Well, you can tell the councilman that my editorial discretion isn't for sale. And Barry? Don't call this line again." Mick slammed the receiver down. The plastic housing cracked with a sharp snap. He stood there for a moment, breathing heavily, staring at the phone as if it were a venomous snake that had just slithered onto his desk.

"Who was it?" Kirri asked, her voice was small.

"Barry," Mick said, lighting another cigarette with hands that shook slightly. "My editor. He just got a call from a concerned member of the Regional Health Board. Apparently, they're worried about the direction of my reporting. They suggested that if I pursue this conspiracy theory, the Herald might lose its biggest advertisers. Specifically, the hospital and the new medical centre." Mick looked at Jinjarli. The triumph was gone, replaced by the grim realisation of what they had just stepped into. "They know we're digging, Jinjarli. And they just fired a warning shot."

"What do we do?" Jinjarli asked. He felt the fear radiating off Mick, a sharp, acidic smell that cut through the stale coffee and toner. Mick took a long drag of the cigarette, the smoke curling around his tired face. He looked at the family tree of money on Kirri's screen, the Redboulder Trust and the NHOA connections, then he looked back at the cracked phone. A slow, stubborn anger began to replace the fear in his eyes.

"What do we do?" Mick repeated. He pulled his chair back into the desk and cracked his knuckles. "We verify the trust deeds. We cross-reference the share prices and then we type until our fingers bleed." He looked up at Jinjarli, a grim smile forming. "They just made a mistake, mate. They tried to scare a journalist. Now, it's not just a story. It's a war."

Chapter 8

Fulgurites and Flow

The studio hummed with a different kind of energy now. The lingering despair was gone, replaced by the fierce focus of an artist possessed by an intense and urgent purpose. The canvases, which had once felt like blank accusations, now seemed to invite exploration, eager recipients of Jinjarli's flourishing understanding. The persistent ache that had plagued him, the quiet heaviness that lingered beneath his skin, still hung on but it no longer stifled his creative fire. Instead, it fuelled it, giving his artistic practice a new, immediate purpose. Jinjarli immersed himself in the raw, tactile process of creation. This was not merely painting; it was the tangible expression of a timeless revelation. He meticulously ground ochre from Country, the deep, vibrant reds that mirrored the basalt of Mount Scoria, the sun-baked yellows and the rich, damp browns of the soil, mixing them with binders to create pigments that felt alive in his hands. Each careful stroke, every calculated blend of earth-derived pigment, was a step deeper into his personal enquiry.

On a large, un-stretched canvas laid flat on the floor, Jinjarli began with sweeping arcs of deep, earthy red, establishing the foundation of the land. From this robust base, he painted fine, almost invisible lines of lighter ochre and white, tracing the subtle, vital flow he'd witnessed on his multimeter. These lines converged and pulsed upwards, coalescing into a human form, its feet firmly connected to the swirling earth. He carefully layered iridescent pigments to suggest the energy, a shimmering current, infusing the figure's body, culminating in a soft, bright aura around its head. This was the electrical potential, the measurable difference, now rendered in a language of form and colour, bringing together the unseen and the seen. Another emerging piece explored the intricate connection of water. He depicted the ancient aquaculture systems of the Gundarra people near Lake Lumina. Within the flowing channels and eel traps, he subtly wove vibrant, almost magnetic patterns. They illustrated how life and energy were nurtured by the precise relationship between people, land and water. He was translating volts into visions and numbers into narratives, turning a scientific anomaly into a testament of ancestral wisdom and living connection.

Weeks drifted by in a haze of ochre dust and the faint scent of linseed oil, Jinjarli losing himself in the developing language of his canvases. He was beginning to feel a shift. One quiet afternoon, as a crisp breeze rustled through the blue gums outside his studio, Kirri called Jinjarli over to the computer.

"You've got a message on your art page; it's from an unfamiliar name, eh, Dr Evelyn Reed?" She clicked it open; a flicker of apprehension mixed with a strange hope whirled around in Jinjarli's stomach. The email was precise, academic and almost clinical in its opening, yet it held an undeniable current of interest beneath its formal veneer. Kirri began to read it aloud:

"Mr Jinjarli, I had the occasion to attend the Hammaholl Health Forum recently. While the official discussion naturally leant towards established protocols and conventional perspectives, I found your presentation... exceptionally compelling. Unconventional, certainly, but compelling nonetheless. I've since had the opportunity to view your online portfolio, particularly your recent works depicting what you term "earth energy" and "disconnection sickness". As a biophysicist specialising in bio-electricity – a field, I might add, that often finds itself on the intriguing fringes of mainstream science – I confess, your artistic interpretation resonates with certain... under-explored avenues in my own research."

Jinjarli felt a jolt, a surge of adrenaline that he hadn't experienced in months. This wasn't another polite, dismissive pat on the head. This was interest, interest from a biophysicist. He leant closer to the screen, as if the sheer force of his gaze could extract more meaning from the words. Kirri continued, her words forming a link between his intuitive world and the rigorous one he was trying to understand.

"Your visual representation of energy flow from the earth to the human body, while presented through an artistic lens, aligns surprisingly well with theoretical models of electron transfer and physiological potential that my colleagues and I have debated for years. I understand from your presentation that you've even conducted some preliminary measurements yourself?" A subtle hint of professional curiosity, perhaps even a gentle challenge, lay buried within that seemingly innocuous question, "However, anecdotal observations, no matter how inspiring, are merely a crucial starting point. To move beyond them and truly engage with the broader scientific discourse, it requires systematic investigation. Rigorous methodology, as Dr Finch so rightly champions." She then transitioned, a subtle but significant shift in tone from intrigued observer to potential collaborator. "If you are open to it, Mr. Jinjarli, I would be interested in discussing your experiences further. More importantly, I believe I could suggest some fundamental scientific avenues to explore. Simple, accessible methods, perhaps involving a bit more than just a multimeter, that could potentially strengthen your observations and lend them the quantifiable "rigour" that the scientific community demands. Think of it, if you will, as translating your profound intuition and ancestral knowledge into a language that the broader scientific community might be willing to understand. A language, perhaps, that even those most firmly grounded in convention might be persuaded to listen to."

Jinjarli reread the email, then again, his fingers tracing the cool, uneven surface of the basalt rock he kept on his table. Under-explored avenues, electron transfer, strengthen your observations. It wasn't the outright, resounding validation he craved, but it was something, coming from a world that had, until now, seemed utterly closed off to his truth. A cautious, yet undeniable, hope-spark ignited within him, chasing away the lingering weariness. This was it. A chance to move beyond whispers and intuition, to perhaps finally speak the language of the Earth in a way that even Dr Finch might be forced to hear.

Jinjarli spent the following three days refining his Earthing Art Project grant application with a fine-tooth comb. It wasn't just a request for funds; it was a manifesto. He had poured his heart into describing how the grant would enable him to expand his use of traditional ochre and natural pigments for new paintings, visually articulating the subtle, vital flow he had detected with his multimeter. He detailed plans for large-scale earthwork sculptures that wouldn't merely depict energy, but would literally draw it from the soil, grounding the art in the very concept it explored. Crucially, he outlined ambitious community workshops, not just for the Gundarra people but for the wider Hammaholl region, aiming to share the basic, accessible principles of grounding. He envisioned elders and children, towns-people and Traditional Owners, all learning together, reconnecting with the land. He pictured the funding allowing for better materials, more accessible venues, perhaps even a small, impactful public exhibition that could genuinely start a conversation. Happy with his application, he clicked submit, a rare, unfamiliar surge of optimism surged through his chest.

The rejection email arrived precisely three weeks later, landing in his inbox like a damp, heavy leaf. It was polite and almost blandly generic,

"Dear Mr. Jinjarli," it began, "Thank you for your application to the Regional Arts Initiative Fund. While we received many strong applications and your project demonstrated unique artistic merit, unfortunately, we are unable to offer funding at this time." No specific reasons. No constructive criticism. No suggestions for improvement. Just a perfectly worded, utterly unhelpful boilerplate refusal. Jinjarli reread it, his brow furrowing. He pulled up his perfectly crafted proposal, scanning its pages for any obvious flaws, any misstep in procedure. There were none. Yet, there it was, a dead end, a polite but firm wall erected with no visible bricks. No obvious explanation. Jinjarli ran his hand through his hair, the vague sense of frustration beginning to gnaw at him again, a persistent whisper that someone, somewhere, didn't want him to succeed.

Kirri, ever the digital watcher, was the first to notice the shift. She had taken to her role as digital drumbeat manager with gusto, diligently helping Jinjarli manage his new online presence. His Earth Pulse Art page on social media was growing, slowly but steadily. Initially, the engagement had been slow but positive. It received a few likes and curious comments from people intrigued by the blend of art and science.

Then, about a week after the grant rejection, the tide turned with an unnerving speed.

"Hey, Jinjarli," Kirri called out one afternoon, holding up her phone with a puzzled frown, her usual bright energy dimmed by a flicker of concern. "You seeing this? Your latest video, the one with you connecting the probe to the basalt from Mount Scoria and showing the voltage drop? It's getting absolutely hammered with downvotes. Like, an abnormal amount for your follower count. Check out these comments." Jinjarli leaned over, his eyes widening in disbelief as he scrolled through the feed. Below the video, a torrent of anonymous comments had appeared.

"Pseudoscience rubbish." read one. "Just another New Age scammer trying to sell crystals to gullible hippies," sneered another. "Where's your PhD, mate? Stick to painting pretty pictures – something you actually understand." What was even more disturbing was the sheer volume of negative reactions, far more than a small, local artist would usually garner. It felt orchestrated, almost. It tasted… manufactured.

"Look at this," Kirri continued, her own fingers flying across the screen, pulling up older posts. "Your previous uploads, even the innocent ones just showing your completed artwork, are suddenly getting negative engagement too. It's not just the new stuff. It's like someone's found your page and is systematically trying to bury it. This isn't just random trolls, Jinjarli. This is... an undertow." Her voice dropped, a rare hint of apprehension in her usually confident tone. "This feels like a campaign. A coordinated effort to discredit you."

The ease with which the online world could be manipulated and the faceless nature of the attacks unsettled Jinjarli deeply. He recognised the strategy as attacking the messenger when the message couldn't be easily refuted. It was a shadowy, insidious resistance, far removed from the direct, if dismissive, arguments of Dr Finch, but equally effective in its chilling attempt to silence. The rejection of the grant now seemed less like an isolated incident and more like a deliberate component of a larger, unseen strategy. Someone, or something, was watching his every move online. And they clearly didn't like what Jinjarli was sharing with the world. The digital drumbeat Kirri had started was being met by a deafening, hostile static. He realised the battle had just moved from a local curiosity to a targeted, professional war.

....

The scent of burning eucalyptus was lingering in the air, a familiar balm against the evening chill. The crackle of the small fire in Uncle Keerray's humble, earth-built hut was the only sound for the longest moment, a deliberate contrast to the distant, unheard buzz of the modern world. Jinjarli sat before his Elder, his clothes carrying the precise acidic tang of cold fear. The frustration of the grant rejection and the digital onslaught still felt fresh. He had sought out his Elder, knowing this quiet space was the only place where the immense weight of his struggle could be properly understood. He laid out the full scope of the resistance. He unloaded the frustration of subtle roadblocks, the grant rejection and the chilling feeling of an unseen hand pushing him back. He spoke of the digital undertow and the systematic effort to discredit him online.

Keerray listened, his face lined with wisdom and the stories of his people. His eyes held a deep connection to the land. They remained steady. He turned a smooth, river-worn stone over and over in his gnarled hand.

"These things you speak of, Jinjarli," Keerray finally murmured, his voice a low, raspy cadence, "they are not new. The shapes change, yes, the tools they use, but the spirit of it… that remains much the same." He stirred the embers with a stick, sending a shower of sparks upwards.

"For centuries, they have tried to tell us our ways were backwards. They called us savage. Our knowledge, our understanding of this Country were called folklore or superstition. They dismiss what they cannot understand, what they cannot control, what they cannot… profit from." He spoke of the immense, deliberate campaigns of cultural erasure. He recalled stories told by his own grandfather, of Traditional

Healers being called witch doctors by the early colonial doctors, their bush medicines dismissed, sometimes even confiscated.

"They wanted us to forget, Jinjarli. To forget what the land gave us, to forget how to listen to its whispers, how to heal ourselves. Because if we could heal ourselves, what need had we for their medicine, their schools, their ways?"

"It's a different kind of fight now, Unc," Jinjarli said, gesturing vaguely towards his tablet. "It's not direct. It's... invisible. Like a shadow." He felt the weariness of fighting a ghost. Keerray nodded slowly.

"Shadows are often the most dangerous, because they make you doubt what is real. This science you speak of, this measuring... it gives a language to what we have always known. Some people do not want that language spoken. It threatens the stories they tell about how the world works and who benefits from it." Keerray picked up the smooth, river-worn stone again. "Do you remember the story of the Koorinya Fire-Healers?" he asked. "This was long ago, before even my grandfather's time, but the story was kept alive, whispered around fires just like this one." Jinjarli leaned closer, always listening with full attention when the Elders spoke, knowing how wise their words were and how ancient their teachings. He closed his eyes briefly, inhaling the smoke, letting the scent pull him into the story.

"In a place not far from here," Keerray began, his voice dropping to a low murmur, "lived a family, the Koorinya. They were known for their ancient healing knowledge... particularly, they knew the secrets of the fire-healing. Not fire to burn, mind you, but the subtle heat of specific stones warmed just so, placed on the body to draw out illness, to calm the spirit, to mend bones. One season," Keerray's voice hardened slightly, "a white doctor arrived, a man of science from the big city. He saw the Koorinya healers working, saw the sick recover and he did not understand. But this doctor... he was not interested in learning respectfully. He saw only something he could take. He took the stones, labelled them primitive tools. He gathered the herbs, called them weeds. He wrote about the quaint superstitions of the natives. Then, he went away. Before he left, he convinced the authorities, with his scientific reports, that the Koorinya healers were unhygienic and dangerous. He convinced the authorities to forbid the fire-healing."

"When a great sickness came later, when their own white medicines failed," Keerray concluded, his eyes holding a deep sadness, "the Koorinya people suffered. The healers, their knowledge suppressed, their tools taken, could not openly practice. The sickness took many. The people here, they felt the cost. They saw their knowledge dismissed, then exploited, then forbidden. This is why we are cautious, Jinjarli. This is why the memory of taking hangs heavy. You are walking a new path, but the old shadows still stretch long." He fixed Jinjarli with a piercing gaze. "Be cautious, Jinjarli. You are walking on sacred ground, yes, but you are also disturbing very powerful nests. Those who benefit from the sickness of disconnection will not give up their hold easily.

Chapter 9

The Lake Lumina Baseline

The video call with Professor Evelyn Reed was a strange blend of the deeply ancient and the cutting-edge modern. It was a collision of two worlds that usually orbited each other in silence. Jinjarli was seated in his Hammaholl studio, the air still thick with the pungent, comforting tang of turpentine and the dusty scent of dry red ochre. He felt small in the corner of the room. He was surrounded by the physical evidence of his struggle: the leaning canvases, the rough chunk of basalt on his table and the yellow multimeter that had started this whole thing. On the screen of his laptop, a window into a different universe flickered. Professor Reed's office was a backdrop of intimidating intellect, whiteboards covered in complex equations, shelves groaning under the weight of thick journals and scientific instruments that looked like polished chrome skeletons. Reed sat forward, her image slightly pixelated by Jinjarli's rural internet connection. Her eyes were bright with a focused intensity that bridged the digital distance.

"Mr. Jinjarli," she began, her voice crisp and analytical. "Thank you for agreeing to this. I have reviewed your initial findings. The 0.03 volts. The 0.07 volts in the mud. It is… promising." Jinjarli rubbed the back of his neck, feeling the grit of ochre dust on his skin.

"Promising is good, Professor. But Dr Finch calls it a placebo. He says I'm just taking a nice walk."

"Dr Finch is operating on a biochemical model," Reed said, waving a hand dismissively. "He looks for molecules. Drugs. I am a biophysicist. I look for energy. What you are observing, this earth energy, aligns with the concept of the Earth's surface being rich with free electrons." Jinjarli frowned, leaning closer to the screen.

"Electrons. Like in a battery?"

"Precisely," Reed nodded. "the Earth has a negative electrical charge. It is essentially an infinite supply of free electrons. Now, the human body… in our modern lives, we are insulated. Rubber shoes. Carpet. Wood floors. We build up a positive charge. We become… static. Think of inflammation in the body, pain, heat, swelling, as a pocket of positive charge that has

nowhere to go. It's a fire with no water to put it out."
Jinjarli stared at the basalt rock on his table.

"A fire," he murmured. "Uncle Keerray talks about the hot sickness. When the spirit is too hot."

"Exactly," Reed said, her voice dropping an octave, becoming less clinical. "When your bare skin makes direct contact, what we call grounding, those free electrons from the Earth transfer to your body. They rush in to neutralise that positive charge. They put out the fire. This isn't mysticism, Mr Jinjarli; it's basic physics. It's potential difference equalising." Jinjarli shook his head slowly. The words were heavy, clunky things. Potential difference. Equalising. They felt cold compared to the warmth he felt on the land.

"Professor, I respect your words. But I'm an artist. I don't see electrons. I see flow. I see the songline." Reed paused. She looked at him, really looked at him, through the screen. She seemed to recalibrate.

"Okay. Forget the physics for a moment. Think of a dam." She used her hands to shape the air. "Imagine a river held back by a great wall. The water builds up, heavy, pressing against the concrete. It becomes turbulent. Stagnant. That is your body in shoes. That is the heaviness you feel." Jinjarli nodded slowly. "Wading through mud."

"Yes. Now, imagine you open the sluice gate. Just a crack. What happens? The water rushes through. It flows. It cleanses the stagnation. It finds its level. That is what happens when you take off your shoes. You are opening the gate. You are letting the lightning of the earth flow into the water of your body." The image clicked. It wasn't numbers; it was nature. The flow, Jinjarli whispered.

"That's what I painted." He stood up suddenly, the chair scraping loudly against the floorboards. "Wait. Can I show you?" He grabbed a canvas he had been working on, the one he had titled The Veins of the Rise. He angled the webcam, struggling to get the lighting right until the glare faded and the image came into focus. It was a large piece, dominated by deep reds and blacks. Running through it were distinct, jagged lines of white ochre that branched out like a river delta or a lightning strike, connecting a central figure to the bottom of the canvas.

On the screen, Professor Reed leaned in so close her nose almost touched her camera. She adjusted her glasses. "Hold it steady," she commanded softly. Silence stretched for a long moment, filled only by the hum of the computer fan.

"That…" Reed started, then stopped. "Jinjarli, look at the branching pattern. The way the white lines diverge from the central point and ground into the darkness at the bottom."

"It's the connection," Jinjarli explained. "The spirit moving down."

"It's a schematic," Reed corrected, her voice filled with wonder. "It's a circuit diagram. That branching pattern? We see that in fulgurites, when lightning hits sand. We see it in the nervous system. You have intuitively painted the path of least resistance. You have depicted the dissipation of electrical charge into a ground plane." She looked up, her face glowing.

"You aren't just painting feelings, Jinjarli. You are documenting bio-electrical observation. You have drawn the physics." A shiver went down Jinjarli's spine. To have his culture's vision validated not just as art, but as science, felt like a physical weight lifting.

"So," Reed said, leaning back, business-like once again. "We have the theory. We have the observation. Now, to shut down Dr Finch, we need the rigour. We need to move from can to does. We need a controlled experiment." She outlined the plan. It was simple but crucial. "Consistency is key. Your multimeter shows voltage potential, which is good. But you need to measure the body voltage. The AC voltage induced in your body by the electrical noise of the modern world, power lines, Wi-Fi, wiring in the walls. When you are ungrounded, you are an antenna, Jinjarli. You are picking up all that noise. When you ground, that noise should drop to near zero." She instructed him to buy a specific Body Voltage Meter. "Secondly, we need a control. You cannot just measure the earth. You must measure the disconnection. You need a comparison.

Measure your volunteers on a rubber mat first. Then on the earth. The contrast is your weapon."

The preparation for the experiment at Lake Lumina the following Saturday was fraught with a specific kind of rural tension. It wasn't a formal scientific expedition; it was a gathering of family. The whole mob would be there and that meant managing personalities. Jinjarli stood by the back of his ute, unloading the gear: the multimeter, the new body voltage meter Reed had insisted on, a stack of heavy rubber car mats he'd scavenged from the wreckers and a clipboard.

"You look like a scientist who got lost at a tip," Murray joked, grabbing the stack of mats. He was playing it cool, but Jinjarli could see the nervousness in his cousin's eyes. Murray was the tech guy; he knew that if the gadgets failed, the embarrassment would be public. Recruiting the volunteers had been the hardest part. Tilly was easy; she was young, eager and believed in Jinjarli implicitly.

"I'm the guinea pig." she'd chirped, hopping into the passenger seat. But the older generation was tougher. Auntie Marra had agreed only after Uncle Keerray had given a silent nod of approval. She stood now by the water's edge, her arms crossed tight across her chest, watching Jinjarli set up. She looked sceptical, her face set in lines of protective caution. She had spent a lifetime being told what was good for her by people with clipboards and she wasn't keen on being a test subject. Then there were the younger men, Jarrah and his mate, Davo. They were leaning against a gum tree, smoking, watching the proceedings with a mix of curiosity and mockery.

"So we just stand on the dirt, Unc?" Jarrah called out, flicking his cigarette butt into a tin. "Is that the big magic? Don't need a degree for that."

"You need to measure it, Jarrah," Jinjarli shot back, trying to keep his voice light. "Can't fix what you can't measure. Just give me an hour cuz."

"An hour of standing around?" Davo laughed. "Hope you got lunch there then Unc."

The scepticism was dense in the air, as thick as the midday heat. They wanted to believe him, Jinjarli knew that. They wanted their ancient stories to be true. But they were terrified that the little yellow box would show nothing, that it would prove Dr Finch right, that it was all just in their heads. The fear of disappointment was a wall between them and the experiment. The sun was high and fierce, beating down on the banks of Lake Lumina. The air shimmered with heat and the flies were relentless. Jinjarli had set up his lab on a flat patch of ground near the reeds: a row of four black rubber car mats laid out on the dry, dusty grass.

"Alright," Jinjarli called out, wiping sweat from his forehead. "Phase one. Everyone shoes off. Stand on the mats." There was a collective groan.

"This rubber is hot, Jinjarli." Auntie Marra complained, stepping onto the black square. She shifted her weight, grimacing. "It's cooking my feet."

"That's the point, Auntie. Just for ten minutes. Please."

The four volunteers, Auntie Marra, Tilly, Jarrah and Davo, stood on their isolated islands of rubber. They were visibly uncomfortable. Without the ability to move or touch the cool earth, the heat seemed to magnify. The atmosphere was agitated. Jarrah was fidgeting, tapping his leg. Davo was swatting at flies with aggressive swipes. Auntie Marra looked like she was about to walk off and go home.

"I feel... dizzy," Tilly said, screwing up her nose. "Like when you rub a balloon on your head. My head hurts."

"That's the static," Jinjarli said, stepping forward with the body voltage meter. "Hold this metal rod." He handed the ground probe to Murray, who stuck it into the earth and handed the sensor rod to Tilly. The meter beeped.

"2.4 Volts," Jinjarli read out. "That's the AC hum in your body, Tilly. You"re an antenna right now." He moved to Jarrah. Jarrah grabbed the rod aggressively.

"Reckon I'm electric, Unc." Jinjarli looked at the screen. It was blank. He frowned. He tapped the screen. Nothing. A cold knot of panic tightened in his stomach.

"Hang on." He wiggled the leads. Still blank.

"Broken already?" Jarrah sneered, though his eyes looked worried.

"Maybe the spirits don't like your machine." Auntie Marra let out a sharp sigh.

"This is foolishness, Jinjarli. We are baking in the sun for a broken toy."

"It's not broken," Jinjarli snapped, his hands shaking slightly. He looked at Murray. "Check the ground probe." Murray scrambled over to where the metal spike was driven into the dry grass.

"It's loose," Murray hissed. "The grounds too dry here. It's not making contact."

"Well fix it." The tension was excruciating. For two minutes, Murray dug frantically with his hands, pouring a little water from his water bottle onto the spike to create mud, jamming it deeper. The volunteers stood on their hot rubber mats, sweating, rolling their eyes. Jinjarli felt the weight of their judgment. He was losing them.

"Try now." Murray yelled, mud on his hands. Jinjarli pressed the button again. The screen flickered to life.

"3.1 Volts," Jinjarli said, letting out a breath he felt he'd been holding for a year. "Jarrah, you"re humming with 3.1 volts of noise." He quickly measured Auntie Marra, 2.8V and Davo, 2.5V. They were all high. They were all stressed, hot and insulated.

"Okay," Jinjarli said, his voice trembling with anticipation. "Step off onto the mud. Right there, by the reeds." The transition was immediate and visceral. As the four of them stepped off the hot, synthetic rubber and sank their bare feet into the cool, dark sludge of the lake's edge, the body language of the group transformed in an instant. It wasn't a subtle shift; it was a complete collapse of tension.

"Oh," Auntie Marra breathed out. It was a sound of pure, unadulterated relief. Her shoulders, which had been hiked up to her ears in the heat, dropped three inches. She closed her eyes, her face tilting up to the sun, but the grimace was gone.

"Oh, that is… that is better."

Jarrah, the joker, the sceptic, stopped moving. He stood ankle-deep in the mud, looking down at his feet. He didn't make a crack about magic. He didn't look at Davo. He just stood there, swaying slightly.

"It's quiet," Jarrah whispered.

"What is?" Jinjarli asked, moving closer with the meter.

"The buzz," Jarrah said, looking up, his eyes wide and vulnerable. "My head. It's usually… loud. Like a radio between stations. It just… stopped." Tilly was giggling, squishing the mud between her toes.

"It's sparkly. It feels like the earth is drinking the headache." Jinjarli approached Auntie Marra.

"Can I measure you now, Auntie?" She nodded, not opening her eyes. He handed her the rod. The meter settled instantly.

"0.01 Volts," Jinjarli read out. The silence that followed was louder than the birds.

"It's gone," Murray whispered, looking over his shoulder. "The voltage. It just dumped."

Jinjarli moved to Jarrah. He held the rod.

"0.00 Volts."

Jarrah looked at the screen, then at the mud, then at Jinjarli. A slow grin spread across his face, not one of mockery, but one of discovery.

"You weren't talking smack, Unc. I'm empty. I'm actually empty." Davo, usually too cool to care, was crouching down, washing his hands in the muddy water.

"It feels like waking up," he muttered. "But, like, actually awake." The group stood there for a long time. The heat of the sun was still there, the flies were still there, but the internal weather had changed. The tension, the inflammation, the static of the rubber mats had been drained away, replaced by the deep, resonant frequency of the land. Jinjarli wrote the numbers down on his clipboard, his hand steady now. He looked at the data: Before – 3.1V. After – 0.00V.

It was just ink on paper. But as he watched Auntie Marra reach out and hold Tilly's hand, both of them grounded in the same mud, he knew it was more than data. It was the bridge. He had used the white man's tool to prove the black man's truth and for the first time, everyone on the bank, from the oldest Auntie to the most cynical boy, could feel the songline humming through them.

"Okay," Jinjarli said softly. "We have the baseline. Now we get to work."

Chapter 10

Inconvenient Anomalies

Dr Lena Petrova lived in a glass box in the sky. Her apartment on the 42nd floor of the Aurora Tower was a masterpiece of modern design, sleek lines, polished timber floors that were sealed with heavy polyurethane and floor-to-ceiling windows that offered a panoramic view of the city's glittering, electric grid. It was beautiful, expensive and utterly insulated. It was 3:18 AM. The digital clock on her bedside table cast a harsh red glow across the room. Lena lay perfectly still under Egyptian cotton sheets that had cost more than her first car. She stared up at the ceiling. Her body was exhausted, heavy with the fatigue of sixty-hour weeks, her mind however, was a frantic, buzzing hive of activity. Her legs ached with a restless, crawling sensation, a low-level inflammation that felt like tiny electrical storms firing in her muscles. She rolled over, the movement stiff and uncomfortable. The silence of the apartment wasn't quiet; it was pressurised. The high-efficiency air-conditioning system hummed a low B-flat that never ceased. The Wi-Fi router in the hallway blinked its rhythmic blue light, a lighthouse warning of nothing. She felt untethered, floating high above the earth, static building up in her cells with nowhere to discharge.

With a groan of frustration, Lena sat up and reached for the drawer in her bedside table. Her hand brushed past a blister pack of Omni-Rest, OmniCorp's flagship sleep aid. She popped the foil, the sound loud in the quiet room and swallowed the small white pill without water. It was her third this week. She knew the pharmacokinetics of the compound intimately; she had led the clinical trials. She knew it would force a chemical shut-down of her GABA receptors, knocking her unconscious but denying her the deep, restorative REM cycles she craved. It wasn't sleep; it was just an erasure of time. She swung her legs out of bed, her feet landing on the plush, synthetic carpet. She walked to the window and pressed her hand against the cold glass. Down below, the city was a grid of amber and white lights, a vast circuit board of humanity. She looked at the park far below, a dark square of void in the sea of light. A strange, illogical thought crossed her mind, a memory of the data she was supposed to be analysing for the upcoming meeting. The barefoot outliers. The people who reported sleeping through the night simply because they touched the ground. Ridiculous, she told herself, the chemical taste of the pill beginning to coat her tongue. It's the placebo effect. It's impossible. But as she stood there, high above the world, vibrating with the accumulated static of modern life, she felt an aching envy for the data points she was about to delete. She wasn't a healer, she realised with a jolt of cold clarity. She was just another broken component in the machine, taking the company oil to stop the squeaking.

....

The gleaming, minimalist conference room on the 27th floor of OmniCorp Pharmaceuticals" City headquarters, usually buzzing with the quiet confidence of impending breakthroughs. Today, however, the air was heavy with a different kind of tension, a subtle, almost imperceptible current of unease that prickled Dr Petrova's skin. As a lead researcher whose brilliance had propelled her rapidly through the ranks, she was accustomed to the hushed reverence for new data. However, this afternoon, seated around the polished obsidian conference table, the data being reviewed felt less like a triumph and more like an inconvenient truth. They were reviewing the preliminary results of a routine, broad wellness trial. This wasn't about a specific drug; it was a fishing expedition, designed to identify emerging health trends and common ailments that could, in the future, be addressed by new pharmaceutical solutions. Lena scrolled through the anonymised participant data on the massive projection screen at the head of the room, her brow furrowing with a familiar intellectual curiosity. The initial findings on sleep quality, chronic pain reduction and inflammation markers for a particular subset of participants were, frankly, peculiar. Startling, even. The group reporting significant, measurable improvements hadn't been on any experimental drug. Instead, their only consistent commonality, buried deep within a self-reported lifestyle questionnaire, was an unexpected uptick in outdoor, barefoot activity. The phrase itself, nestled innocuously, had almost been flagged for removal by the automated data cleaner as an irrelevant outlier.

Marcus Howell, Senior Vice President of Global Strategy and the room's undisputed gravitational centre, leaned back in his ergonomic chair. A faint, almost unnoticeable smile played on his lips, a carefully cultivated expression that rarely reached his shrewd, calculating eyes.

"Interesting anomalies," he murmured, his voice as smooth and polished as the conference table's surface. "Highly subjective, of course. Self-reported anecdotal improvements. We'll need to run those numbers through a more robust filter. Perhaps a larger sample size, specifically focusing on... verifiable metrics that align with our current research pipelines." His gaze, sharp and direct, flickered to Dr Lena Petrova.

"Dr Petrova, your team handles the statistical analysis, yes? Ensure we're isolating any... extraneous variables that might skew the overall picture. We must maintain our focus, mustn't we?" The implication was clear, though unspoken: these unexpected results were not breakthroughs; they were inconvenient noise. Another senior researcher, Dr Chen, a man whose career had been built on aligning research outcomes with corporate objectives, chimed in,

"Indeed. And the financial implications of pursuing avenues outside of our core competencies... well, that's hardly a responsible use of shareholder funds, is it?" He glanced pointedly at a slide detailing OmniCorp's impressive projected quarterly earnings, a silent reminder of their collective purpose. Lena watched the data shrink on the screen, feeling a cold knot form in her stomach. It wasn't an explicit suppression of findings, not yet. It was more sophisticated, almost elegantly insidious. A quiet, almost telepathic consensus was forming around the table to simply reframe or de-emphasise any data that didn't point directly towards the development of a new, patentable drug. The phrase benefits outside of pharmaceuticals hung in the air, unsaid but undeniably lingering, like an inconvenient ghost in the machine. It was scientific truth being subtly, deftly, steered away from the path of profit, a path Lena had always believed in, until now. The very notion of a free, natural intervention was repellent to OmniCorp's business model.

Later that day, the sterile hum of the biostatistics lab felt kind of oppressive. Lena found Dr Marie Shroder, a long-time colleague and trusted confidante whose wry humour often cut through the corporate veneer, meticulously recalibrating a complex machine. Marie's face was illuminated by the diagnostic screen's glow, her usual animated expression replaced by a tight-lipped focus.

"Marie," Lena began, her voice low, almost a whisper against the background drone of the machinery. "Did you see the raw data from that wellness trial? The barefoot correlations?" She watched for a reaction. Marie paused her adjustments, her shoulders stiffening almost uncomfortably. She didn't look up immediately, instead she pressed a final sequence of buttons. When she finally spoke, her voice was tight and purposefully neutral.

"I did. Remarkable, isn't it? For self-reported data." She finally turned, her eyes meeting Lena's and Lena saw the same flicker of unease, the same gnawing discomfort that had been eating at her own conscience since the meeting.

"Remarkable isn't the word Howell and Chen seemed to prefer," Lena retorted, a hint of bitterness in her tone that surprised even herself.

"More like inconvenient anomalies to be filtered out before the final report." Marie sighed, a sound that held years of unspoken frustrations, a weariness beyond the day's work.

"It's the unspoken directive, isn't it?" she mused, walking over to the coffee machine and pouring two lukewarm cups that tasted more like cold regret than caffeine.

"We're here to find problems that our products can solve. Not to confirm that solutions might exist elsewhere, especially if they're... free, or worse, natural." She pushed a cup into Lena's hand. "How many times have we seen it, Lena? A promising compound that doesn't quite fit the blockbuster profile, so it gets shelved. Or research that hints at a simpler, less profitable intervention gets quietly... re-prioritised out of existence." Lena took a sip of the bitter coffee, its warmth doing little to thaw the cold knot in her stomach.

"This feels different, Marie. The scale of it. The way they just omitted those correlations in the draft report, almost before they were even acknowledged. It feels like a deliberate turning away from something genuinely beneficial, simply because it doesn't align with the financial model. With Marcus Howell's profit projections." Her voice dropped even lower, tinged with a new kind of fear. "What if this earthing Jinjarli talks about, this unbroken songline... what if it's real? What if it could help people on a scale we can't even touch with our most expensive drugs and it costs nothing but bare feet on the earth?" Marie leaned against the counter, her gaze distant, fixed on the sterile white walls of the lab.

"Then we're not just researchers, Lena," she said, her voice barely audible. "We're part of the problem. And I'm not sure how much longer I can be part of that."

The silence that followed was heavy, filled with the unspoken weight of their shared scientific integrity and the looming, profitable shadow of OmniCorp.

Outside, the city lights of the City centre began to twinkle, millions of tiny connections, oblivious to the subtle, vital disconnection being fostered within the walls. The public debate at the town hall had been a maelstrom of words, a storm of clinical terms from Dr Finch and a cascade of questions from the community. It had left Jinjarli feeling bruised and exhausted. The sheer volume of verbal noise a was painful opposite to the quiet wisdom of the land. His paintings, for all their vibrant ochre, felt contained, a truth trapped behind a frame. He needed to speak a language they couldn't dismiss, a language of soil and stone and living earth. He needed to make a songline they could all see and touch.

....

The digital clock on the bedside table read 3:14 AM. The numbers glowed a harsh, aggressive red in the absolute darkness of the master bedroom. To Alistair Finch, the silence of his home usually felt like a sanctuary, a testament to triple-glazed windows and high-grade insulation. This night, however, the silence was heavy, pressurised, broken only by the ragged, shallow breathing of his wife. Hazel was curled into a tight feotal ball on her side of the bed, her knuckles white as she gripped the silk pillowcase. She wasn't sleeping; she was enduring.

"Hazel?" Alistair whispered, his voice sounding loud in the stillness. She flinched. A tiny, involuntary spasm.

"Light," she gasped, her voice a dry rasp. "Too bright." There was no light. The blackout blinds were drawn tight, sealing them in a tomb of expensive darkness. Alistair knew the physiology of a cluster migraine. To Hazel, the firing neurones behind her eyes were creating their own strobe light, a jagged aura of pain that blinded her from the inside out. Alistair threw back the covers and stood up. His feet sank into the plush, deep-pile carpet. He moved with the efficiency of thirty years of medical practice, navigating the room by memory. He went to the en-suite bathroom, the motion-sensor nightlight flicking on, a soft, amber glow that he knew would feel like a knife in Hazel's eyes if she saw it. He cracked the door only an inch.

He opened the medicine cabinet. It was arranged with the precision of a pharmacy. He bypassed the paracetamol, the ibuprofen, the mild sedatives. He reached for the lockbox on the top shelf. His fingers, usually steady enough to suture a facial laceration without a tremor, fumbled with the combination. Left to 4. Right to 12. Left to 9. Click. He withdrew a blister pack of Rizatriptan and a small vial of injectable Pethidine. This was the heavy artillery. The break-glass-in-case-of-emergency protocol. He drew up the syringe, checking the dosage against the light. 50mg. Standard protocol for acute, intractable pain. He returned to the bedroom.

"Hazel, darling. I need you to turn over. Just a little." She whimpered, a sound of pure, animal distress.

"It's… splitting, Alistair. It's splitting open."

"I know. I know." He sat on the edge of the bed. The mattress, an ergonomic memory foam marvel designed for perfect spinal alignment, absorbed his weight silently. "This will help. It has to help." He administered the injection. Efficient. Clinical. A small sting, then the plunge. He waited.

In the hospital, this was the moment the patient's shoulders would drop, the moment the chemistry overtook the biology and forced the body into submission. He checked his watch. The luminous dial hovered in the dark. Five minutes. Hazel groaned. Ten minutes. She began to rock back and forth, a rhythmic motion of agony. Twenty minutes.

"It's not working," she choked out. She rolled onto her back, pressing the heels of her hands into her eye sockets until Alistair worried she might bruise the tissue. "Why isn't it working? You said this was the strong one."

"It takes time, Hazel. Give it a moment to bind to the receptors."

"It's been months, Alistair. Months of waiting for it to bind." Her voice cracked, rising into a sob that was cut short by a fresh wave of nausea. She scrambled up, stumbling blindly toward the bathroom. The sound of her retching echoed off the Italian marble tiles, a harsh, violent noise that shattered the sterile peace of the house. Alistair sat frozen on the edge of the bed. The syringe sat on the nightstand, an empty plastic tube. A useless piece of plastic.

He stood up and walked out of the bedroom, closing the door softly to muffle the sound of his wife's suffering. He walked down the hallway, his bare feet making no sound on the polished timber floorboards of the living room. The house was perfectly climate-controlled, set to a constant 21 degrees, yet he felt a chill seeping into his bones. He entered the kitchen, a cavern of stainless steel and quartz. He didn't turn on the main lights; the ambient glow from the street lamps outside filtered through the sheer curtains. He poured a glass of water from the filtration tap, chilled, purified, stripped of all minerals and drank it in one gulp. It tasted of nothing. He leaned against the island bench and looked at the wall opposite. There, framed in tasteful matte black, were his credentials. The Bachelor of Medicine. The Fellowship of the Royal Australian College of General Practitioners. The awards for Service to Rural Health. The certificate of his appointment to the Regional Health Oversight Committee. They hung there in the shadows, glass rectangles reflecting the blinking blue light of the Wi-Fi router in the corner.

He looked at his hands. These hands had set bones. They had stitched wounds. They had signed thousands of prescriptions that sent people to the pharmacy with the promise of relief. Yet, twenty feet away, the woman he loved was vomiting from a pain he couldn't touch, couldn't measure and couldn't stop. He felt a vibration under his feet. The refrigerator compressor kicked in. A low, rhythmic thrum-thrum-thrum. Usually, he ignored it. Tonight, in the silence of his failure, it felt like the house was vibrating. A low-frequency assault. He looked at the floor, engineered timber over a concrete slab, over moisture membrane, over polymer seal. Layers. So many layers.

"A wall," he whispered. It was an accusation, he knew. Walls were necessary. Walls kept the roof up. Walls kept the wind out. He had spent his life fortifying the human body against entropy, using chemistry to impose order on the biological chaos. If he took the wall away... if he let the flow in... what else would come in with it? He was terrified that if he acknowledged the energy Jinjarli spoke of, he would be admitting that the universe was wilder, stranger and more uncontrollable than his textbooks allowed. He wasn't just protecting his reputation; he was protecting his understanding of reality.

A wall between your feet and the breathing earth. The words of the old Aboriginal man, Keerray, floated into his mind. He pushed them away immediately. Ridiculous, his training snapped back. Superstition. Placebo. As the sound of the toilet flushing echoed from the master bedroom, followed by the soft thud of Hazel collapsing back into bed, Alistair Finch stared at his degrees and realised that for all his science, tonight he was just a man standing in a box, holding a glass of dead water, listening to his wife cry.

Chapter 11

The Hunting Ground

The idea was born during a quiet walk with cousin Murray by Lake Lumina. The sun was setting. As it dropped below the horizon, it painted the water in purple and orange hues. Jinjarli felt a powerful surge of energy through his bare feet. It wasn't a number on a multimeter; it was a feeling, an intense sense of connection. He just wanted to share it.

"It's not just a feeling, Murray," he said, pointing to the ground. "The land… it has a pulse. A story that runs under the surface, like veins." Together, they began the work on a secluded rise near the water's edge. The scale of the project was daunting. It was not a sculpture of rock, but of the very land itself. They began to dig, not with heavy machinery, but with simple tools, shovels and small spades, a respectful exchange with the earth. It was hard, physical work that left Jinjarli's muscles aching, but it was a good ache, a feeling of being in deep communion with Country.

Over the next seven weeks, a powerful image began to emerge from the red soil. They carved a massive, sweeping form that resembled a human figure lying on the land, its feet reaching toward the water's edge. From the figure's core, a series of bold, flowing lines radiated outward, following the natural contours of the rise. They were like the arteries of the earth, the veins of a living body. The lines were a visual representation of Jinjarli's discovery. They were a picture of the energy he had measured. Jinjarli filled the trenches with alternating layers of vibrant red and white ochre from his studio, making the lines of the songline pop against the dark soil.

The work was slow and tedious. Murray, with his logical mind, helped with the measurements, ensuring the lines were straight and the proportions correct. He saw the project as a monumental, living data set. Well, it was. Jinjarli with his hands the colour of dirt, saw it as a kind of meditation. He always worked barefoot, feeling the soil beneath his feet as he shaped the form of the giant figure. Inevitably, the piece attracted attention. A few local birdwatchers and dog walkers were the first to stumble on it. They stopped, their expressions a mix of confusion and awe. Soon, a local news crew arrived, led by the familiar, slightly rumpled figure of Mick Davies. Mick had been following Jinjarli's story, but this was different. This wasn't just a controversial idea or a scientific anomaly; this was a visible, undeniable act of creation.

"It's beautiful, Jinjarli…," Mick snorted, his voice full of genuine admiration as he stood at the edge of the rise, his camera crew filming from a distance, "…what is it?"

Jinjarli stood within the finished figure. The dirt was clinging to his hands. He looked up, not at Mick, but at the sky.

"It's what our people have always known," he said simply. "It's a songline. A visual story. It shows the connection. We are not just on the land. We are part of it. We are the veins, Mick."

The story ran on the local evening news. The earthwork, with its powerful symbolism and stark beauty, became a national talking point. Some saw it as a beautiful piece of land art. Others saw it as a provocative statement. Either way it was a very public challenge to the very idea of a world built on pavement and disconnection. The art was no longer contained within the walls of his studio; it was out in the open, on sacred ground, inviting everyone to step onto the earth and feel its pulse for themselves.

Auntie Tarni felt a familiar prickle of irritation as she walked the track by the lake. She'd heard the whispers, seen the photos on young Tilly's tablet, Jinjarli's great big artwork, a sculpture of raw dirt and ochre. The talk in the community hall had been a collection of hope and apprehension. It was a debate she thought had been settled generations ago. She belonged to the old guard, a group whose memories of dispossession and forced assimilation ran deep. Her scepticism was a shield. Formed as a necessary armour against a world that had always found a way to take and twist their stories. Her heart was a fortress built of hard-won caution and she was here to see this so-called living sculpture for herself. She was fully prepared to find it a cheap, hollow spectacle.

When she crested the rise, her words hitched in her throat. She expected a messy, amateurish pile of dirt. Instead, she found a powerful, deliberate statement. The earthwork, carved into the land itself, was vast, an immense human figure lying in profound communion with the soil. The ochre lines, vibrant reds and sun-baked yellows, followed sweeping, confident arcs, radiating from the figure's core and reaching toward the water. It wasn't a painting or a statue; it was an act of belonging. A small crowd had gathered. An old man stood at the edge, a hand resting on the smooth bark of a red gum. His head tilted as if listening to the roots. Children with faces smeared with ochre, ran barefoot through the lines. Their laughter was a joyful, uninhibited sound. A young mother sat nearby, holding her baby. She traced a pattern in the dirt with her finger, a quiet teaching moment unfolding before Auntie Tarni's eyes. This wasn't a protest. It was a reclaiming. Auntie Tarni's gaze fell on a single line of white ochre that traced its way from the figure's foot to a patch of rich, damp earth. Her mind, so quick to recall the past, brought up an image of her own mother, who had been punished as a child for speaking their language in a white-run school. This art, this very line, was speaking a language the modern world couldn't censor. It was here, on their land and it was undeniable.

The doubt arrived not as a dramatic lightning bolt, but as a soft, persistent whisper. It was a crack in the fortress. She thought of Elder Keerray's words, a voice as old as the hills themselves. A wall between your feet and the breathing earth. The sculpture was not just a representation; it was the physical embodiment of that wisdom. It wasn't about a white man's tool or a cheap number on a screen. It was about what was underneath it all. It was about the fact that her feet, her people's feet, were no longer on asphalt. Auntie Tarni took a slow, deliberate step onto the earthwork. The soil was cool and firm beneath her bare feet, a solid connection that she hadn't realised she'd been missing. She walked a few paces, the ochre dust clinging to her soles, feeling the subtle shift in the ground. She looked at the children, their joyous faces smeared with the colours of Country and felt a profound, unexpected welling of pride. This was not a giving away of their knowledge; it was a sharing. It was a lesson being told in a new way, with the same ancient truth at its heart.

She stood there for a long moment, the quiet buzz of the community around her and the deep, silent song of the land beneath her. She hadn't come here to be changed. But as the sun dipped low, casting long shadows from the sculpted earth, Auntie Tarni realised her scepticism, once her greatest strength, had a small, hopeful crack running right through it.

The bustle of local success was a warm, unfamiliar feeling. Mick Davies' segment on the nightly news had been a tremendous triumph. The camera had lingered on the ochre-and-earth lines of the earthwork, painting a powerful image that spoke a language beyond words. The phone in Jinjarli's studio was usually quiet, now ringing constantly with calls from community members, well-wishers and even a few curious artists from outside the region. The feeling of being understood and of having his truth seen, was a soothing balm after the fiery debate at the town hall. The real battle though, was being fought in silence, in a digital world that Jinjarli barely understood. Kirri was the first to notice the undertow. She perched at her desk, in her small office, a small corner of the community centre. Her fingers danced across the screen with an almost alien dexterity. She wasn't just checking Jinjarli's social media; she was his digital guard. She tracked his online footprint. It was late in the week following the Earthwork launch when Kirri saw it. It wasn't a single, direct attack. It was a coordinated campaign. It was a subtle chorus of voices and they were all singing the same off-key tune.

Kirri pulled up a series of articles and blogs, the URLs filled with a deceptive normalcy: Wellness Watchdog, Scientific Sense, Holistic Health Forum. The articles were not outright condemnations. They were more insidious. They began with a polite acknowledgment of Mr Jinjarli's commendable artistic expression and charming cultural perspective. The beauty of his earthwork was commended; however, the pivot came as a subtle knife, twisting the narrative.

While his art is compelling, his claims remain firmly in the realm of anecdote, one article read, its tone formal and condescending. We must caution against attributing clinical results to what is, at best, a New Age trend. Science demands measurable, repeatable data, not a romanticised view of our ancestors beliefs. Another article, filled with scientific jargon, used the words pseudoscience and unsubstantiated claims to dismiss his theory. They called his multimeter readings flukes, easily influenced by electromagnetic interference from power lines. They took Elder Keerray's wisdom, which they referred to as folklore, and presented it as a kind of quaint superstition. They used his very identity as a weapon, framing his truth as a cultural relic that was out of place in a modern world. It was a well-funded, professionally executed effort to discredit him without ever making a direct, provable accusation. Jinjarli read them in silence, the quiet triumph of the earthwork now a sour taste in his mouth.

This was a new kind of wall, a digital one, far more difficult to scale than the town hall's polished walls. He felt the sickening shame of being labelled a fraud. Jinjarli's cousin Murray, ever the pragmatist, was furious.

"This is ridiculous. It's all speculation and half-truths. There are no names, just faceless articles from websites no one has ever heard of."

"That's the point," Kirri said, her voice tight with a cold fury. "You can't argue with a ghost. They are designed to look independent, but they are all using the same language, the same talking points. It's like a corporate memo was passed around to a hundred different bloggers." She ran a quick background check and found a digital breadcrumb, a single shared IP address for three of the sites. The address belonged to a small PR firm in City that had a track record of working for... big pharmaceutical companies. The web of ownership Mick had discovered now had a name and a face, however small it was.

The weight of it settled on Jinjarli's shoulders. This isn't just a difference of opinion. He wasn't just fighting a doctor and a sceptical community. He was fighting a much larger, more powerful shadow. They were threatened by a truth that couldn't be packaged or sold. He looked at the multimeter on his desk. The numbers were small, yes, but they were real. He looked at his hands, still stained with the ochre of the earthwork and he felt the unshakeable truth beneath his skin. They had tried to paint his ancient knowledge as superstition. Now, he would paint their greed as a sickness. The town hall meeting was no longer just a forum for debate; it was a stage for a larger fight. He would go, not to plead his case, but to expose the digital wall they were building.

The world outside Kirri's office was asleep, a silent, unmoving canvas of darkness. But inside, her screens cast a pale, flickering glow on her face and her mind was a whirlwind of frantic energy. The community hub was a quiet place at this hour, the only sound the low hum of a server and the rhythmic click of her mouse. She felt like a digital tracker, following a ghost through a vast, dark forest. She started her hunt not with a bang, but with a whisper. Three of the most venomous articles she'd found, the ones that had used the words pseudoscience and folkloric nonsense, had been posted within minutes of each other, all from different domains. That was no coincidence. She dove into the deep web, searching for breadcrumbs. The domain names themselves were a dead end, all cloaked behind anonymous registrars. But the hosting provider data was a different story.

After hours of painstaking cross-referencing and poring over a dozen different IP address logs, she found it. A single, shared and very well-hidden server cluster. It was the same digital fingerprint on all three sites. She was so close. She began to poke and prod at the cluster, looking for any flaw, any open port, anything that would give her a name. The suspense built as the hours bled into one another. The screen was a maze of code and data, a language only she could read. She wasn't just looking at text anymore; she was seeing a motive, a shadow. The deeper she went, the more cold and deliberate the whole thing felt. This was not a bunch of random internet trolls. This was a professional job, designed to look random. Just before dawn, she found the seam. A single, carelessly left link on a deep forum, a connection that tied the server cluster to a small shell company in a tax haven. She knew the game now. She started digging for the shell company's registered agents and directors. She was working on a hunch, a gut feeling that had nothing to do with code and everything to do with Uncle Keerray's wisdom.

Then, there it was. A name. A director, listed for the shell company. A quick search of the name on LinkedIn and professional databases confirmed it. The director was an employee of a City-based PR firm called The Busguardian Group. She began to follow the money, looking for The Busguardian Group's clients. Their client list was confidential, but a quick search of their public press releases and case studies showed a pattern. They worked with major corporations in the health and wellness space, often helping to manage public perception during a crisis. A crisis, she realised with a chilling clarity, like a new, unscientific therapy that was gaining traction, one that offered a cure that cost nothing. She cross-referenced the names of their former executives with the local news article Mick Davies had written about the web of ownership.

The connections were everywhere. She looked at her screens, the glowing maze of data now a clear, horrifying picture. Jinjarli wasn't fighting an idea. He was fighting a business model. A multi-million-dollar industry that saw his truth as a threat. The battle wasn't just for his art. It was a fight for the very right to say that a free, natural remedy could exist. Kirri picked up her phone, her fingers trembling slightly. It was 5:15 in the morning. She didn't care. She had to tell Jinjarli. The quiet hum of her computer filled the silence and her voice was a hoarse whisper.

"I found them."

Chapter 12

Returning to Source

Uncle Moray's hands were not just tools; they were archives. They were broad, dark and mapped with the topography of seventy years of hard work. The pads of his fingers retained a sensitivity that defied the calluses. He knew the language of bone and sinew, of fever and fatigue. His morning rounds were a ritual of frustration. He walked the familiar streets of the mission housing, his boots crunching on the gravel. His first stop was Uncle Lionel's place. Lionel was a man who had spent forty years shearing sheep and now his joints were paying the price with interest. The small living room smelled of camphor oil and stale tea. Lionel sat in his armchair, his leg propped up on a milk crate, his face grey with pain.

"Morning, Moray," Lionel grunted, trying to shift his weight. "She's biting today." Moray knelt, ignoring the groan of his own knees. He placed his hands gently on Lionel's swollen knee. Through the fabric of the trousers, he could feel it, the heat. It wasn't just inflammation; to Moray, it felt like a trapped fire, a chaotic, static energy buzzing beneath the skin, looking for a way out but finding none. He began to massage, using the old techniques, pushing the fluid, trying to encourage the flow. He could feel the resistance. The body was a closed loop. The heat moved, but it didn't leave. It just swirled around, angry and trapped.

"I can move it, Lionel," Moray murmured, his brow furrowed in concentration. "But I can't drain it. The pills the doctor gave you?"

"Make me sick in the gut," Lionel said, waving a hand at a bottle on the table. "And the pain is still there, just… further away. Like a dog barking in the next yard." Moray finished up, washing his hands in the kitchen sink. He looked out the window at the asphalt road, the concrete footpath, the rubber-soled slippers Lionel wore. He felt a deep, simmering helplessness. He was a healer whose tools were failing because the world had changed. The connection was broken and all he was doing was pushing the pain around inside a sealed container.

Later that afternoon, Moray stood in the shadow of a River Red Gum near the lake, watching

Jinjarli and Murray working on the earthwork. They were laughing, holding that yellow plastic box, the multimeter. Moray crossed his arms. He loved his nephew, but this… this was art. This was performance.

"Measuring dirt," Moray muttered to himself, shaking his head. "How does a number fix a knee like Lionel's?" To Moray, healing was sweat, heat, oil and touch. It was physical. Jinjarli's talk of volts and electrons sounded like white fella magic. Cold, invisible and useless for a man in pain. He saw the ochre lines, the beauty of the sculpture and while his spirit appreciated the respect for Country, his healer's mind saw it as a distraction. You couldn't paint away arthritis. You couldn't sculpt away insomnia. He turned to walk away, dismissing the yellow box as a toy. But as he turned, he saw Jarrah, one of the young fellas, step onto the wet mud near the sculpture. He saw the boy's shoulders drop. He saw a physical shift in his posture that Moray recognised instantly, the release of tension. Moray paused. He looked back at the multimeter sitting on a rock. Curiosity, the healer's oldest companion, pricked at him. He waited until dusk. The sun had dipped below the horizon, painting the sky in bruises of purple and orange. Jinjarli and the others had packed up and gone home for a feed. The earthwork was silent. Moray walked up the rise. He felt foolish, like a man trying to catch the wind in a net. He spotted the multimeter where Jinjarli had left it, tucked under a protective tarp. He picked it up. It felt light, cheap. He fumbled with the dial, turning it until the screen blinked to life with a series of zeros. He remembered what he'd seen Jinjarli do.

He sat down heavily on a large, dry rock. He kept his heavy work boots on. He pressed the black probe into the dirt. He pressed the metal tip of the red probe against his thumb. The numbers danced. 2.1V. 2.3V.

"Noise," Moray grunted. "Just noise." Then, he leaned forward. He unlaced his boots. He peeled off his thick wool socks. The cool evening air hit his skin. He placed his bare feet flat onto the damp red earth of the sculpture. He watched the screen. The numbers didn't just change; they collapsed. 2.3V... 1.0V... 0.05V... 0.00V. Moray blinked. He lifted his feet. 2.2V.

He put them down. 0.00V. He sat there for a long time in the growing dark. He wasn't looking at a voltage reading. He was looking at a confirmation. The heat he felt in Lionel's knee, the buzzing he felt in his own hands after a day in town, the machine saw it too and the earth took it.

"It's not art," he whispered to the silence. "It's a drain."

The conversion wasn't just about numbers; it was about witnessing the change in his people. Two days later, Moray was walking near the reeds when he found Jarrah again. Jarrah was twenty-two but he carried himself like an old man. He worked construction and his back was a knot of constant spasms. Usually, Jarrah was restless, unable to sit still because of the low-grade pain firing in his lumbar. Today, Jarrah was lying on his back in the centre of the earthwork, his arms spread wide, his bare heels dug into the clay. He was asleep. Moray approached softly. He watched the boy's chest rise and fall. It was a deep, rhythmic beat. Moray knelt and gently touched Jarrah's shoulder. Jarrah woke with a start, then relaxed when he saw the Elder.

"Sorry, Unc. Dozed off."

"How is the back?" Moray asked. Jarrah sat up. He twisted his torso left, then right. A look of genuine confusion crossed his face.

"It's… quiet. Usually, it's screaming by this time of day. It feels cool. Like someone put ice on the inside."

"The earth is breathing the pain out of you," Moray said, not as a metaphor, but as a diagnosis. But the true miracle was in Auntie Marra's kitchen. Marra had been the community's insomniac for a decade. Grief and worry had wired her brain; she walked the floors at night, a ghost in her own home. Moray had given her bush teas, the doctor had given her pills, but nothing kept her under for more than an hour. Moray visited her three days after she had started her morning routine of sitting barefoot in her garden. The house was quiet. Usually, the radio was blaring to cover the silence, but today it was off. Marra was sitting at her table, a cup of tea in her hand, staring at the wall clock.

"Morning, Marra," Moray said, letting himself in. She looked at him and her eyes, usually rimmed with red and shadowed by dark circles, were clear.

"Moray," she whispered, pointing at the clock. "Look at the time." It was 8:00 AM. "I went to bed at ten," she said, her voice trembling. "I sat in the garden yesterday evening like Jinjarli said. Just feet on the dirt for twenty minutes. I felt… heavy. Good heavy. I went to bed." She looked at him, tears welling up. "I didn't wake up, Moray. I didn't hear the possums on the roof. I didn't worry about the bills. I just… went away and I came back now." Moray reached across the table and took her hand. Her skin felt cool, calm. The frantic, nervous vibration that usually hummed under her skin was gone.

"You slept," Moray said.

"I slept," she confirmed. "Real sleep. The kind that knits you back together."

That evening, the fire in Elder Keerray's hut was a low, crackling heart in the centre of the room. Uncle

Moray sat across from him, the silence between them deep with new understanding.

"He has a gift, that boy," Moray finally murmured, his voice a low rumble. "He has found a way to show what we have always felt." Keerray nodded slowly.

"The songlines were not all sung with voices, Moray. Some were written in the land itself." Moray leaned forward, the firelight catching the deep lines of his face.

"I tested the yellow box, Keerray. I took it to the earthwork when no one was looking." Keerray raised an eyebrow but said nothing. "It saw the heat," Moray admitted. "It saw the noise leaving the body and I have seen the people. Auntie Marra slept through the night. Jarrah's back is cool to the touch. They tell me of the feeling of it, of the quiet strength that flows from the earth." He paused, wrestling with his pride. "I thought the healing came from the mind, from the stories or from my hands alone. But he has shown me that it comes from the land. A physical flow. A current.

The box just gives it a number."   Keerray's lips twitched into a small, knowing smile.

"You are a healer of the body, Moray. I am a healer of the spirit. We have always known that the body and the spirit are one. What he has done is to show the young ones, whose minds are filled with the new ways, that the healing is real. That it is a language with numbers." The healer shook his head, a flicker of doubt in his eyes.

"But the tool, Keerray. The plastic box. Is it not… a desecration? To reduce the spirit to a digit?"

"Is a song a desecration because we write it down on paper?" Keerray countered softly. "The white man's tools are just that, tools. The knowledge they bring is neutral. He is not replacing our way, Moray. He is strengthening it. He is building a bridge so the young ones can walk back to us."

Moray sat in silence for a long moment. He thought of Lionel's swollen knee, of the heat trapped inside. He thought of the 0.00V on the screen. He realised he had been refusing a tool that could help his people simply because it was made of plastic. He reached out and gently rested a hand on Keerray's arm.

"He needs our help, then," Moray said, his voice quiet but firm. "The town hall will be full of words. They will bring their own numbers. Their own science. Jinjarli has the volts, but he doesn't have the patients."

"Then you will speak their language," Keerray said. "No," Moray corrected him, standing up. "I will show them the results. I will track the healing. I will write down the sleep, the pain, the heat. I will make a map of the body to match his map of the land." He walked to the door of the hut and looked out at the stars. "We will show them that our songline is not broken. It has just begun to be heard."

Chapter 13

The Hostile Pavement

The idea was Mick Davies', a calculated move in the chess game of public opinion. He'd seen the power of Jinjarli's art on the news, the silent argument of the earthwork.

"We need to go bigger," he had told Jinjarli. "We need to take the message from the bush and put it right in the heart of town." The concept was simple, but audacious. A public, barefoot walk down Hammaholl's main street, followed by a communal art display in the town square. It was a direct, physical challenge to the sanitised, concrete world that had caused the sickness in the first place.

It was held on a Saturday morning and the weather held. The sun was actually a warm blanket and a gentle breeze rustled the leaves on the street's old trees. The crowd gathered slowly. A nervous energy was in the air. It wasn't just the Gundarra people. People from all walks of life were arriving. There were young families, older couples, university students and a handful of curiosity-seekers who had read Mick's stories in the Herald. They stood at the starting point, an unspoken question in their eyes: Are we really going to do this?

Jinjarli stood at the front, his ochre-stained hands holding a small, polished piece of basalt. He was no longer just an artist; he was a leader. Beside him stood Murray, his tablet ready to record and behind him, a small but sturdy group of elders, including Uncle Keerray and Uncle Moray, their presence a silent and powerful blessing. Kirri moved through the crowd, her phone a constant flash of light, documenting every face and every nervous smile. The art display was set up on a patch of public grass. It became a temporary gallery of Jinjarli's work. His paintings showed figures with their feet on the earth, their bodies radiating with vibrant energy. The multimeter sat on a small stand, its bright yellow casing a stark and deliberate statement.

Then, they began. The first step was the hardest. The concrete was rough and cold underfoot. It was a strange, vulnerable feeling to walk a public street without the usual armour of shoes. Some people winced, others walked gingerly but as the crowd moved, a shift began to take place. The initial awkwardness gave way to a quiet, shared purpose. The rhythmic slap of bare feet on pavement created a new sound in the urban environment, a subtle drumbeat that echoed a feeling older than any building. They turned the corner onto Hammaholl's main street and the texture of the world changed.

For Jinjarli, who had spent the last weeks acclimating to the soft loam of the lake and the cool grass of his backyard, the main street was an assault course. The asphalt, baked by the morning sun, radiated a dull, thrumming heat that seeped instantly into the soles of his feet. It wasn't the living warmth of the sun-baked rock at Mount Scoria; it was a dead, chemical heat, smelling of tar and oil. He looked down at the river of feet moving beside him. It was a mesmerising sight. Pale feet, dark feet, calloused feet and the tender, unblemished feet of office workers who hadn't touched the ground in years. They moved in a syncopated rhythm, a soft slap-slap-slap that sounded like rain falling on the road. But the city fought back.

"Watch out." Murray called out, pointing to a glitter of diamonds on the road ahead. Broken glass from a beer bottle, shattered and scattered near the gutter. The crowd rippled, parting around the hazard like water flowing around a rock. Jinjarli stepped gingerly. His foot came down on something hard and sticky, a wad of chewing gum, black with grime, cooked into the pavement. He winced, feeling the synthetic intrusion against his skin. Further along, cigarette butts lay like toxic confetti and the metal covers of utility grates buzzed with the electricity running beneath them. This wasn't just a walk; it was a revelation of hostility. They were realising, with every step, just how incredibly unwelcoming their own habitat had become. The city was built for tires and rubber soles, not for flesh. Yet, there was power in it. The vulnerability of their bare skin against the harsh street made the act of walking together feel brave. They were soft things in a hard world, reclaiming the space one step at a time.

They walked past shops with gleaming windows. They passed cafés filled with people in shoes. They passed the very building where Dr Finch had dismissed Jinjarli's claims. The doctor himself was not there, but Jinjarli felt his presence. As if a ghost of disapproval hung in the air. The air was so thick you could taste it. The police presence was a quiet yet observing force. Evidence of the official world unable to comprehend what was happening. The walk culminated in the town square. A small stage had been set up and Mick, along with a cameraperson, stood by, ready and excited. Jinjarli stepped onto the stage, the warmth of the sun was a solid presence on his back. He didn't speak of volts or diagnoses. He spoke of his heart.

"They say there is a sickness of disconnection," he began, his voice clear and strong. "They say we need medicine to cure it. I say the cure is here." He gestured down to his own bare feet. "The earth has a pulse. An energy. Our ancestors knew it. They never lost the feeling." He spoke of Uncle Keerray's wisdom, of the community's healing, of the simple truth that could not be dismissed.

"This walk... it is not just for us. It is for all of humanity. It is a songline. A path back to a truth that has been waiting for us all along." A ripple went through the crowd. This was not a protest. It was an invitation. The air in the town square was no longer thick. There was a new, collective breath lingering in the air. Jinjarli, surrounded by his people and his art, knew this was the new beginning. The truth was no longer just a flicker on a multimeter. It was becoming a movement.

Dr Alistair Finch observed the procession from the cool, quiet security of a café window on Hammaholl's main street. The glass was clean, a perfect shield between him and the messy spectacle outside. He had come here not out of curiosity, but out of a professional sense of duty. He had a need to bear witness to what he considered a public charade. The air inside the café smelled of roasted coffee and antiseptic hand sanitiser, a familiar, comforting blend of efficiency and hygiene. The world outside, however, was a chaotic mess. The stench of car fumes, body odour and yesterday's regrets was clogging the air. The first thing he noticed was the dust. It rose in small, unhygienic clouds with every step of the barefoot walkers, a fine, gritty haze that seemed to cling to the clean asphalt. He watched with a small, professional frown on his face as the marchers moved past. It was exactly as he had predicted: a group of well-meaning but misguided individuals, wrapped in the comforting blanket of unscientific folklore. He catalogued them in his mind with pure clinical precision: a few local families, some new-age types, a handful of teenagers clearly there for the spectacle. Harmless, if not slightly ridiculous.

All of a sudden Dr Finch's professional detachment began to fray. He saw a man he recognised. It was one of his own patients, a man he had prescribed a mild sedative for a recurring anxiety he couldn't seem to shake. Here the man was smiling, his face a picture of genuine, unprescribed calm. He saw a woman he had seen at the local hospital board meetings. She was a woman of impeccable logic and poise and was now walking barefoot with a look of quiet liberation. The doctor's gaze settled on the art display in the town square. He dismissed the ochre paintings as a pleasant, if somewhat primitive, aesthetic. But the multimeter, sitting on a stand next to the vibrant art, bothered him immensely. It was an instrument of pure, quantifiable science, being used as a prop in a performance of intuition. It was a corruption of the very language of his world. Then, he saw Jinjarli on the stage. He didn't hear the words, but the images on the local news feed he pulled up on his phone spoke volumes. Jinjarli, his feet stained with the dirt of the land, spoke with a conviction that Dr Finch couldn't dismiss as mere enthusiasm. He heard a sound bite that echoed with unsettling clarity: "They say there is a sickness of disconnection…"

The phrase, so simple and unscientific, hit him with a cold jolt. He himself had spent his life in sterile rooms, surrounded by data and machines. He lived in a house with manicured lawns and concrete paths, completely insulated from the natural world. He had spent his entire career diagnosing ailments he could see, symptoms he could measure, but what about the vague, unnamed ailments of the modern world? The fatigue, the anxiety, the sense of un-wellness that so many of his patients felt, a feeling he himself, if he were to be honest, had occasionally felt. He had always prescribed a pill for it, a chemical solution to an unquantifiable problem. He watched the marchers disperse, their bare feet now covered in the dust of the street, their faces alight with a shared purpose. They were a movement of feeling, a living contradiction to his world of logic and data. He had no logical argument to counter them, no numbers to disprove the look of peace on his patient's face, no diagnosis for the silent unease that had now settled in his own heart. The wall of his professional certainty, once so impenetrable, not anymore.

....

The newsroom of the Hammaholl Herald was a place of controlled chaos, but for Mick Davies, that evening was different. The silence was deafening, punctuated only by the soft click of his mouse. He sat in front of his computer, a half-empty coffee mug beside him, staring at the finished article. He had checked every fact, verified every record and re-read every quote. It was ready. The culmination of weeks of digging, of following Kirri's digital breadcrumbs and his own professional instincts. With a deep breath that had nothing to do with lukewarm coffee and everything to do with a quiet sense of destiny, he hit the publish button. The article, titled Barefoot Prophet and the Web of Ownership, went live.

The piece started with Jinjarli's story, the unscientific barefoot walk and the profound community response it had inspired. It was a compelling, human hook. But then, the tone shifted. Mick's pen, which had previously chronicled the quirky and the local, now sliced through the professional façade of power. He laid out the facts, one by one. He revealed the interconnected directorships, a tangled financial web that linked local health officials to regional investment funds. He named the key players, including a subtle but damning section on Dr Finch's board memberships. He detailed how those same investment funds held significant, though often obscured, shares in major pharmaceutical companies like OmniCorp and VitaGlobal. The article was a meticulously constructed argument, showing how individuals in positions of public trust stood to gain from the very healthcare model they espoused. It was not a claim of conspiracy, but a presentation of conflict. Mick's words were precise, analytical and utterly devastating. He hinted at a larger systemic issue, suggesting that when the very people tasked with public well-being have a financial stake in a specific kind of medical solution, the patient's best interest might be lost in the transaction. He ended with a simple, provocative question: What if the cure for our modern ailments is so simple, so free, that it can't be sold?

The phone at the Herald office began to ring. An elderly woman called, her voice trembling with gratitude. A young man called, furious and demanding to know how they could have allowed this to happen. The noise began to build, a low, electronic roar. The article was shared, then shared again. It wasn't just a local news story anymore; it was a digital wildfire.

In a well-appointed home across town, Dr Alistair Finch's phone buzzed with an urgent text. He read the article, his face draining of colour. The polite, professional facade he had so carefully constructed for decades had been torn down by a local journalist. He felt a cold fury, a terrible fear that this one, audacious act would bring down his entire carefully built world.

....

Later that evening, in the quiet of Jinjarli's studio, the phone rang. It was Mick.

"It's out," he said, his voice flat with exhaustion and a quiet sense of triumph. "And it's not going away." The war of ideas had just moved into a very public arena and the rules of the game had just changed. Mick's article didn't just land; it detonated. The quiet town of Hammaholl became a battle ground of whispered arguments and heated social media posts. The controversy was no longer contained in a sterile town hall or an anonymous forum; it was in the checkout lines at the local supermarket and over cups of tea at the community hall. One-half of the town felt vindicated. People who had quietly believed Jinjarli's story now spoke up. An elderly woman who had suffered from chronic pain for years wrote a letter to the editor, recounting how just ten minutes of walking barefoot in her garden each morning had made a difference. Younger people, who had felt a vague sense of disconnection, were now talking openly about their own struggles and how Jinjarli's art and message had resonated with them. The narrative of disconnection sickness had found a name, a diagnosis and a community ready to embrace it.

However, the other half was outraged. The town council and prominent business leaders, particularly those with ties to the healthcare sector, condemned the article as a baseless attack on their integrity. Dr Finch, his professional reputation now publicly questioned, went on the local radio, his voice a measured baritone of condemnation. He called Mick's article an unsubstantiated conspiracy theory and a dangerous piece of amateur journalism that risked eroding public trust in legitimate medical science.

The pressure on Mick was immediate and intense. His phone was a constant buzz of angry voicemails and his newspaper's publisher was fielding calls from furious advertisers. Just when the local pressure felt overwhelming, the phone on Mick's desk rang with an unfamiliar number. He answered, his voice weary.

"Mick Davies?" a voice on the other end asked, clipped and professional. "This is Rebecca from the Sydney Morning Herald." Mick's heart pounded. The Sydney Morning Herald was one of the largest news outlets in the country.

"Yes, this is Mick."

"Hello Mick. We've been following the story about the artist, Jinjarli and the earthing theory. The local controversy, your article on the financial connections... well, it's caught our attention. It's got all the hallmarks of a major story on the intersection of public health, corporate influence and Indigenous knowledge." Rebecca wasn't interested in the local gossip. She was interested in the systemic issue. She wanted to know about the web of ownership, the role of Dr Finch and most importantly, Jinjarli and his theory. She wanted to fly out a team to interview

Jinjarli, Uncle Keerray and others from the community. They wanted to do a major feature, a long-form piece that would put the story on the national stage. After Mick hung up the phone, a mix of elation and dread settled over him. This was what every journalist dreamed of. A story with national reach. It was also a story that would put Jinjarli, his family and his entire community under a level of scrutiny they had never known. The local battle for a single town's soul was about to become a very public, very high-stakes war for a nation's.

The community hub was usually a sanctuary of low-humming servers and the comforting scent of ozone and dust. For Kirri, it was her cockpit. It was 2:00 AM. The rest of Hammaholl was asleep, dreaming under the heavy blanket of the night, but Kirri was wired on caffeine and the glow of three monitors. She was scrubbing the comments section of Jinjarli's latest video. It was tedious work, blocking bots, deleting the same copy-pasted vitriol about snake oil but it was necessary. She was the gatekeeper. Suddenly, her Spotify playlist, a heavy rotation of 90s hip hop, cut out. Silence slammed into the room. Kirri frowned, tapping her mouse.

"Hello? Wi-Fi?" Her main monitor flickered. Not a glitch. A pulse. It went black, then flashed white. Then black again. A window opened on her desktop. It wasn't an email. It was a root-access terminal command, the kind that shouldn't be appearing unless she was typing it herself. Green text began to scroll, typing itself character by character.

Then it just blinked. Once. Twice. Then, an image resolved. Kirri's breath hitched, trapping a scream in her throat. It wasn't a server log or a trace route. It was a photograph. Grainy, taken from a distance, but unmistakable. The peeling paint on the front gate. The overgrown wattle bush.

It was her house.

A second image popped up beside it. A playground. Children in uniforms blurring in motion. In the foreground, focused with terrifying clarity, was the back of a small head with messy braids. Tilly. The adrenaline didn't come as a rush; it hit her like a physical blow, cold and sickly. Her hands, usually so steady on a keyboard, began to tremble. This wasn't a warning. It was a promise. The message beneath the images was simple text, stripped of any hacker bravado: WE KNOW WHERE YOU SLEEP. WE KNOW WHERE SHE PLAYS.

"They aren't just watching the network," Kirri whispered, the silence of the room suddenly deafening. Every shadow felt occupied, every creak sounding like a footstep. "They're watching us."

She slammed the laptop shut, the snap echoing like a gunshot. The technical details, the hops, the IP masking, didn't matter anymore. The digital wall she had built around herself had been breached, not by superior code, but by brute intimidation. Kirri ripped the ethernet cable out of the wall followed by the power cords. The room fell into darkness. She sat on the floor. This wasn't trolls. This wasn't an algorithm. Someone was inside her life. They knew where she slept. They knew where Tilly went to school. She grabbed her phone, her fingers trembling so hard she could barely unlock it. She needed to call Murray. She needed to get Tilly. But as she stared at her phone screen, a notification banner slid down from the top. It was a text message from an unknown number.

Don't call the police. We own the network. Go back to sleep, Kirri.

She threw the phone across the room, It hit the far wall with a crack. She pulled her knees to her chest in the dark, listening to the hum of the refrigerator, realising for the first time that the digital world she loved wasn't a playground. It was a hunting ground and the fences were down.

....

Three days after the photo incident, Kirri was operating like a ghost. She was using a burner laptop she'd bought for cash at a pawn shop two towns over. She was tethered to a prepaid 4G dongle, sitting in the back of Murray's ute parked on a fire trail, miles away from any fixed IP address associated with her family. She wasn't hiding anymore. She was hunting.

She was on the dark web, navigating a Tor forum known for hosting whistleblowers and hacktivists. She had posted a canary trap, a specific, coded plea for help buried in the metadata of a viral cat video she knew the opposition's bots were scraping. It was a long shot. A desperate shot. A private message appeared in her encrypted inbox. The sender ID was GhostProtocol.

GhostProtocol: You need to improve your OpSec. The cat video was clever, but they flagged it in 40 seconds. Kirri typed back, her breath fogging in the cold air of the ute cab.

Who is this?

GhostProtocol: Someone who is tired of writing the code that ruins your life. Kirri hesitated. It could be a trap. A way to trace her location. She checked her

VPN status. Double-routed through Panama and Estonia. She was safe-ish.

Kirri: Prove it.

A file transfer request appeared. She accepted it. She opened the file. It was a log of the attack on her computer three nights ago. It showed the exact timestamp, the script used to bypass her firewall and the command to print the document. But it also showed something else. The Origin IP.

"Kirri: You were the one who hacked me?"

"GhostProtocol: No. I'm the one who scrubs the logs so the boss doesn't go to jail. That was a freelancer. "BlackHat_44". Hired by a subcontractor."

"Kirri: Why are you telling me this?" There was a long pause. The cursor blinked.

"GhostProtocol: My mum has rheumatoid arthritis. She saw your brother's video. She started sitting in the garden. She... she walked to the mailbox yesterday without her cane. First time in two years." Kirri felt a lump form in her throat. The songline was working. It was reaching even the people paid to destroy it.

"GhostProtocol: I work for a firm called The Busguardian Group. We are contracted by a shell company owned by Horizon Investment. They are running an Astroturf campaign. Fake grass roots."

"Kirri: I know that. I can't prove it."

"GhostProtocol: I can."

Another file transfer came through, this one was massive. Kirri opened it. It was a presentation. The title slide read: OPERATION DISCONNECT: Neutralising the Indigenous Narrative via Algorithmic Saturation. She scrolled through it. It was sickening. It detailed everything. The persona profiles for the fake bots. The script for the concerned doctors. The budget for the ReConnect pill marketing. The specific instructions to target Jinjarli's family to induce psychological fatigue. It was a smoking gun. It was a nuclear bomb.

"Kirri: This is... this is everything."

"GhostProtocol: It's enough to hang them. But you can't use it just yet. The metadata is tagged to my user profile. If you leak this PDF, they will know it was me."

"Kirri: So what do I do?"

"GhostProtocol: You don't leak the document. You use the document to find the server farm. They are running the botnet out of a legitimate data centre in Quay-lands. If you can ping that server from your end and log the response time, you can prove the bots and the PR firm are on the same physical hardware. That's public proof. That's legal."

"Kirri: Where is the server?"

GhostProtocol gave Kirri the server address, "The password for the back door is ProfitOverPeople. Go get em, Kirri. Tell your brother... tell him thanks for my mum." The connection severed. GhostProtocol went offline. Kirri sat in the darkness of the bush, the blue light of the laptop illuminating her fierce grin. She wasn't the victim anymore. She had the map.

Chapter 14

Operation Disconnect

The dawn light usually brought Kirri peace, but today it revealed a nightmare. She stood at the edge of the earthwork, her boots sinking into the mud. Beside her, the Elders stood in a silence that was heavier than grief. It wasn't graffiti. There were no spray-painted tags or crude slurs. This was precise. Surgical. A heavy trench had been cut straight through the centre of the ceremonial ring. It was the width of an excavator bucket, the edges sharp and compressed. The ancient arrangement of stones, which had mapped the stars for generations, hadn't just been scattered; they had been crushed. Pulverised into gravel and compacted into the mud by heavy machinery.

"This wasn't kids," Uncle Vic said, his voice trembling with a rage he was fighting to control. He pointed to the tracks, deep, wide treads that spoke of industrial equipment. "Look at the lines. Straight. Efficient."

Kirri walked to the edge of the trench. It was a professional demolition. Someone had hired a crew, signed a work order and paid an invoice to erase this history. It was a corporate flex, a demonstration that to the people they were fighting, this sacred ground was just dirt to be moved.

"They didn't want to vandalise it," Kirri said, feeling the bile rise in her throat. "They wanted to delete it."

Someone had scraped away the vibrant red and white ochre from the veins of the figure's torso, leaving a raw, wounded gash of dark soil. The beautiful, flowing lines, the arteries of the living earth, had been smeared and gouged out. Even more chillingly, a single, straight line of stark black spray paint had been added, cutting across the figure's heart. It was a cold, geometric intrusion on the organic form, a line of lifeless logic on a canvas of living truth. As she walked closer, a gut-wrenching fear took hold. Just above the figure's ankle, in the very place where Jinjarli had connected the multimeter's probe, a single, thick-soled work boot lay on the dirt. The rubber sole, dull and insulating, faced the sky. It was a clear, brutal reference to Uncle Keerray's wisdom, an undeniable statement. We know your story and we are going to tear it down.

When Jinjarli stood over the desecration, his hands clenched into fists, trembling with a fury so cold it felt like ice. This wasn't just vandalism. This was a violation. They had entered his sacred space, desecrated his art and mocked his deepest beliefs. He was no longer fighting a war of words or ideas. He was fighting a shadow that was willing to cross a line, to make a statement that was both deeply personal and chillingly professional. He fell to his knees, his own hands, still stained with ochre, touching the raw wound in the soil. The pulse of the earth felt distant, muted by the cold fear that had now settled in his bones. The peaceful, spiritual journey was over. He was at war now. For the first time, Jinjarli realised just how much he had to lose.

....

The fire in Uncle Keerray's hut was a low, murmuring presence, its glow the only light in the space. The air was still and pungent. The scent of burning eucalyptus lingered. Jinjarli walked in, his clothes carrying the stains of his fractured hope. He said nothing. He didn't need to. He simply stood there, his hands clenched into fists, the last remnants of ochre on his skin a stark reminder of the desecrated earthwork. Uncle Keerray's gaze passed over the ochre and landed on the cold dread in Jinjarli's eyes. He didn't need to be told. He knew.

"Come, child," he said, his voice a low, raspy murmur. "Sit. Let the fire's warmth reach you." Jinjarli sank onto a small mat on the earthen floor. He spoke then, the words tumbling out in a rush, of the scraped earth, the gash in the living lines, the single black line of paint and the boot. The words were a frantic search for a meaning that felt beyond comprehension. Keerray listened in silence, his face etched with deep lines that held the memory of every hardship his people had endured. When Jinjarli finished, a long moment passed. The fire crackled softly.

"I am not surprised," Keerray finally said, his voice as quiet and firm as the rocks outside. "We have walked this path before, my boy. When the white man came and saw our medicine, they called it superstition. When they saw our art, they called it primitivism. When they saw our knowledge, they called it folklore. They dismiss what they cannot understand. But what happens," he continued, his gaze piercing, "when they cannot dismiss it? When they try and the truth of it still shines through? That is when they try to break it. To erase it." He gestured with a gnarled hand toward Jinjarli's still-trembling hands. "You did not just make a sculpture. You made a wound in their world. You showed them that their sickness has a name and that the cure is free. You have disturbed a powerful nest, Jinjarli. You are a light, a beacon and a small flame in a great wind that wants to snuff you out." An immense sadness settled in his eyes. It was not a sadness for the earthwork, but for the heavy burden Jinjarli had chosen to carry.

"For centuries, they have tried to erase our connection to this land. With laws, with fences, with schools, with their own stories. Your art, this earthing, is a song they do not want to hear. Now, they are trying to silence the singer." He reached out and gently rested a hand on Jinjarli's knee. "They are not just attacking your art, my boy. They are attacking you. They are afraid of the truth you carry. They are afraid of the people who are starting to listen. Be cautious. Be watchful. But know this," Keerray said, his gaze unwavering, "…you are not alone. The story you tell is ancient. It is our story. We will not let them silence it." The fire crackled and in its warmth, Jinjarli felt the full weight of the danger. The fight for his truth had come at a heavier price than he ever could have imagined.

After the raw fear of the day's vandalism, Jinjarli felt a powerful urge to retreat. He wanted to pull away from the public eye and tend to the wound in the earthwork. He had ignored his phone, his laptop and the incessant humming of the world beyond his studio walls. Murray and Kirri, with her quiet, insistent patience, wouldn't let him.

"You can't let them win by being silent," Kirri said. "The digital static, the hate, it's a message. But so are these." She gestured to the laptop. "These are from the people who are listening." Hesitantly, Jinjarli opened his inbox. The messages, a torrent of them, were overwhelming.

They came from every corner of the globe, written in a dozen different languages that his browser automatically translated. They were not from fellow artists or scientists, but from people from all walks of life. A farmer from the American Midwest wrote about a persistent back pain that had plagued him for years.

"I read your story about the barefoot thing and tried it myself. Just to see. My pain ain't gone, but it feels… different. Less angry. I walk my fields now without shoes and it's like the land is breathing my pain away." A programmer in Tokyo, whose world was a maze of fluorescent lights and endless code, described a similar sense of disconnection. He had felt a strange, quiet peace after a friend suggested he walk barefoot in a small public park.

"Your art gave me a name for this feeling," he wrote. "The songline is not just for your country. It is for the whole world." A young woman from Europe, suffering from a chronic ailment that doctors couldn't diagnose, shared her story of a quiet, powerful energy she felt when sitting barefoot in her garden.

"I thought I was making it up," she wrote, "but your words gave me courage." As he scrolled, Jinjarli felt the weight of his fear begin to lift, replaced by a sense of wonder. The messages were a universal language of shared experience. The concrete cage was not just a local confinement. The deep current was not just a cultural metaphor. This was a universal, physical reality. It was not through a doctor's chart or a scientific paper. These people had found this truth through an intuitive, personal resonance with the earth. Jinjarli was no longer a lonely artist with a crazy idea. He was a small though vital part of a global awakening. The powerful forces who had tried to silence him with vandalism and professional smear campaigns had miscalculated. Their actions had only amplified his voice. Had only sent it to people who in their own way were already looking for the same truth. He looked at the screen. It was a new kind of songline, connecting him to strangers thousands of kilometres away. The threats were real. So was the truth. A truth that could not be silenced.

Chapter 15

The World Chorus

The studio looked like NASA mission control, if NASA was run on a shoestring budget and red ochre. Kirri didn't look at the screen as a grid of pixels; she looked at it as a landscape. To the uninitiated, the scrolling green code was just data. To her, it was scrub. Dense, tangled and hiding things that bit. She sat in the back of the ute, the blue light of the laptop illuminating her face like the moon. She wasn't hacking; she was tracking. She was looking for a disturbance in the digital dust.

"They think they're invisible," she murmured to Murray. "But everything leaves a track. Even a bot." She typed a command line. It wasn't a keystroke; it was a spear throw. She sent the packet out into the dark web, watching it bounce off the satellite nodes.

"The server farm isn't a fortress, Murray," she said, her eyes narrowing as she watched the latency numbers spike. "It's a waterhole. It's where the predators gather to drink. You just have to wait downwind." She watched the cursor blink. It was hovering over a masked IP address in the Docklands. The connection was encrypted, wrapped in layers of

SSL security like a Wait-a-While vine, designed to tangle you up until you starved. But Kirri knew the bush. She knew that even the thickest vine had a root.

"Found the game trail," she whispered. "Look at the packet loss. That's a footprint. Heavy traffic. Clumsy. They're moving money, not just data." She bypassed the firewall, slipping through the digital fence line just as her ancestors would have slipped through the boundaries of a pastoral station. She was inside. The directory listing sprawled out before her, not as a list of files, but as the skin of the animal she had been hunting.

"We got the pelt," she said, hitting the screenshot key. "Now let's see whose wall it hangs on. We have to do this fast," Kirri said, her voice tight. She was typing with both hands, her eyes darting between screens.

"GhostProtocol gave us the coordinates, but once we ping the server, their sysadmin is going to see us. We have maybe three minutes before they cut the connection or trace us back." Murray stood behind her, holding the multimeter like a talisman.

"What exactly are we doing, Cuz?"

"We are tracking an animal," Jinjarli said from the corner. He wasn't looking at the screens; he was sharpening a piece of charcoal. "Kirri is finding the tracks."

"Exactly," Kirri said. "I'm running a trace route. I'm going to send a packet of data, a digital message, from here to the IP address the mole gave us. I'm going to map every hop it takes. If it lands on the same rack of servers that hosts the Busguardian website and the fake wellness blogs and the bot army... we have them." She pulled up a visualisation tool on the main screen. It was a map of the world, dark, with lines of light connecting cities.

"Ready?" Kirri asked. Her finger hovered over the Enter key.

"Go," Murray said. She hit the key.

On the screen, a red line shot out from Hammaholl. It hit a node in Melbourne. Then Sydney. Then it bounced to a satellite. Then back to a secure data centre in Melbourne's Quay-lands.

"Come on," Kirri whispered. "Open the door."

A terminal window flashed. LOGIN REQUIRED.

Kirri typed: User: Admin. Password: ProfitOverPeople.

The screen froze. A spinning wheel of death.

"They changed it," Murray groaned. "The mole gave us an old password."

"No," Kirri said, her eyes narrowing. "They didn't change it. The system is hesitating. It's a honey trap. They're watching us." Suddenly, a map on the second screen lit up. Red dots began to swarm around their location.

"They're backtracking the signal." Murray yelled. "Pull the plug."

"Not yet." Kirri shouted. "I'm inside. I just need the directory listing. I need to screenshot the folder structure." Her fingers flew. ls -la /var/www/html/ clients. Text flooded the screen. It was a directory of every client hosted on that server.

"Gotcha," Kirri hissed. It was all there. The corporate giants and the independent hate blogs, all sitting in the same digital bedroom, holding hands.

"Kirri. The trace is at 90%." Murray warned. "They're hitting the ISP."

"Screenshotting... one... two... three..."

Kirri hit Command+Shift+3 repeatedly. The shutter sound echoed like gunfire.

"NOW." Kirri screamed.

Murray yanked the main power cable from the wall.

The screens died instantly. The hum of the cooling fans whined down into silence. The room went pitch black. For a moment, nobody breathed. The only sound was the thumping of their own hearts and the distant cry of a mopoke owl outside.

"Did we get it?" Jinjarli asked from the dark. Kirri fumbled for her phone and turned on the flashlight. She shone it on the battery-powered laptop she had kept off the main grid. She flipped the lid open. There, on the desktop, were five PNG files. The directory listing. The smoking gun that proved the PR firm, the pharmaceutical company and the hate mobs were one and the same entity. Kirri slumped back in her chair, wiping sweat from her forehead. She looked at her brother.

"We got them," she said, a fierce, trembling smile breaking across her face. "We just tracked the biggest predator in the bush and we brought back the skin."

Jinjarli stepped into the light. He placed a hand on the cold plastic of the laptop.

"Good tracking, Sis," he said softy. "Now, we give the skin to Mick Davies. And tomorrow, we hang it up for the world to see."

. . . .

The email from Professor Evelyn Reed arrived like a lifeline. It was concise and professional however, beneath the academic language, Jinjarli could sense a current of genuine excitement. It wasn't a request for a meeting; it was an invitation to a meeting already in progress. The subject line simply read:

Your Observations & Global Corroboration. He clicked the link and his laptop screen filled with a grid of faces from different time zones. From different worlds. He saw Professor Reed, her eyes bright with a focused intensity. Beside her was a woman with a no-nonsense demeanour and a tired but hopeful expression, Dr Amaria Kerma, a name he recognised from Mick Davies's reporting. A third figure was a man with a neatly trimmed beard and calm eyes, Dr Eli Vustergaard, a researcher from a bio-lab in Sweden. The conversation began immediately, a beautiful, complex dialogue that wove his spiritual truth into the fabric of their scientific inquiry.

"Mr Jinjarli," Professor Reed began with a quiet respect in her voice,"what you have measured with your multimeter isn't just an anecdote. It is a very real phenomenon. The Earth's surface is rich with free electrons, which possess a negative electrical charge. We've been theorising about a direct transfer to the human body, your work provides some of the most compelling visual and anecdotal evidence we have seen." Dr Kerma spoke next. Her voice was full of a weary conviction.

"I've been tracking your story, Jinjarli. You've put a name to something we've seen for years. Our research at OmniCorp hinted at it, but the data was always suppressed. The correlations between barefoot activity and reduced inflammation, improved sleep... they were considered inconvenient outliers because there was no profitable product to attach them to. You've given us the courage to step out of the shadows."

The conversation was a breathtaking intellectual dance. Jinjarli spoke of Elder Keerray's wisdom, the unbroken songlines that connected his people to the land. Dr Vustergaard responded by showing them images of his research. The intricate bioelectrical maps of the human body and the subtle ways they react to natural environments. He spoke of the Nordic tradition of walking in the forests. He showed various healing properties of the natural world.

"Your truth is not just your own, Jinjarli," he said, his voice calm and firm. "It is a universal human truth. We have found it in our own ways and now, we have found each other." They outlined a plan. It would be a global, collaborative study. Professor Reed would handle the academic rigour, designing a new methodology that could stand up to any scientific scrutiny. Dr Kerma would use her knowledge of corporate research to anticipate their opposition's arguments. Dr Vustergaard would coordinate the international data collection.

"We will prove it," Dr Kerma said with a fierce determination in her eyes. "We will create a body of evidence so large, so undeniable, that no one will be able to dismiss it as an anecdote." The isolation Jinjarli had felt after the vandalism evaporated. He was no longer a lone artist fighting a corporate shadow. He was now a vital part of a global team. The threats were real, but so was the truth and it was a truth that had just found a worldwide chorus to sing it.

Chapter 16

The Permission to Run

Dr Finch sat in his clinic the leather of his ergonomic chair creaking like a dry branch. He had two more patients to see. Across the desk sat Mrs Gable, a woman of seventy-four whose hands trembled with a familiar, rhythmic palsy. She was waiting for her script. Alistair looked down at the pad of paper. It was premium stock, cream-coloured and heavy. He gripped his Montblanc pen, an instrument of weight and balance that had cost more than Mrs Gable's entire fortnightly pension. He uncapped it. The ink was black and permanent.

"Just the usual refill, Doctor," Mrs. Gable said, her voice thin and reedy. "The sleeping ones. And the ones for the shakes." Alistair lowered the nib to the paper. The tip touched the line where his signature belonged. Alistair J. Finch, MD. He told his hand to move. It didn't. A sudden, claustrophobic heat bloomed inside his Italian leather shoes. The laces, tied in a perfect double knot, felt like wire garrottes cutting off the circulation to his metatarsals. He could feel the blood pooling in his feet. It became stagnant and angry. He tried to write the A. His fingers spasmed. The pen skittered sideways, leaving a jagged, ugly scar of black ink across the cream paper.

"Doctor?" Mrs Gable asked, leaning forward. The air conditioner hummed, a relentless, recycled thrum that seemed to vibrate in the fillings of his teeth. It smelled of ozone and dust mites, a dead air that had been breathed by a thousand sick people before him. He looked at Mrs Gable's hands. Then he looked at the bottle of pills on his shelf. They weren't medicine anymore. They were silencers. He was prescribing silence to a woman who was screaming on the inside. He dropped the pen. It hit the desk with a clatter that sounded like a gunshot in the sterile room.

"I can't," he whispered, the words scraping his throat. "I... I need to check the dosage."

He pushed his chair back, the wheels rolling on the plastic mat, insulated from the floor, insulated from the earth, floating in a sea of static. He needed air. He needed dirt. He needed to get these constricting shoes off before they crushed the bones of his feet.

. . . .

The boardroom on the 47th floor of The Busguardian Group building was not a place of evil; it was a place of suffocating, hermetically sealed order. The air conditioning hummed a low, persistent and monotonous drone, a sound that drilled into the base of the skull after three hours. The room smelled of nothing, literally nothing. The air had been scrubbed, filtered and ionised until it was just a cold, invisible gas. Ben Huntley, the lead strategist, didn't look like a shark today. He looked like a man who was eroding. His tie was loosened, revealing a neck raw from the starch of his collar. He stood before the massive screen, rubbing grit from his eyes. He hadn't seen the sun in three days. Seated around the obsidian table were the representatives from OmniCorp and VitaGlobal. They weren't leaning back in arrogance; they were slumped in exhaustion. Marcus Howell, the VP of Strategy, was staring at his tablet, his face bathed in the blue light of a stock ticker that was trending relentlessly downward.

"The numbers aren't holding, Ben," Howell said, his voice quiet, devoid of threat, filled only with the heavy gravity of a quarterly report. "The barefoot trend... it's not just the fringe anymore. I have shareholders asking why our sleep aid sales are down 4% in the APAC region. 4%. Do you know what that does to my blood pressure?"

Huntley sighed, tapping the remote against his palm. He looked out the floor-to-ceiling window. The city below was a grid of grey and glass, millions of people rushing nowhere.

"It's the narrative, Marcus," Huntley said, turning back to the room. "Jinjarli is selling them something we can't manufacture. He's selling them time. He's telling them to stop. To breathe. To touch the dirt."

"We can't sell stop," the VitaGlobal executive murmured, massaging his temples. "The economy runs on go. If people stop, the whole machine grinds to a halt. We have a responsibility to keep them functional."

Ben Huntley paced the plush carpet of the conference room, tapping a remote against his palm. On the screen, a casting sheet for the ReConnect commercial was displayed.

"Exactly," Huntley said. He clicked the remote. The screen changed. It didn't show a weaponised attack plan; it showed a mood board. Soft greens, clean lines, a woman in a business suit pausing to look at a tree.

"We don't fight the artist," Huntley said, his voice tired. "We help him. We take his messy, impractical truth and we package it into something people can actually use. Because let's be honest, gentlemen... who has time to walk barefoot in the mud? Who has time to sit in a pit of leaves?" He gestured to the woman on the screen. She looked stressed. She looked tired. She looked exactly like everyone in the room.

"She has a mortgage," Huntley said softly. "She has two kids in private school. She has a commute. She has high cortisol and low serotonin. She doesn't want a revolution, Marcus. She just wants to sleep. She wants the noise in her head to stop. She just can't afford to take her shoes off to do it." He clicked the button again. The image of the ReConnect pill bottle appeared. It wasn't glowing or sinister. It looked clean. Efficient. A small, manageable mercy.

"We aren't tricking them," Huntley reasoned, believing his own words. "We are offering a compromise. We are distilling the essence of the earth into a format that fits in a handbag. We are giving them the permission to keep running, because the world doesn't let them stop." Howell looked at the bottle on the screen. He reached for his glass of water, his hand shaking slightly, a tremor of caffeine and stress. He took a sip. The water was chilled, purified, dead.

"The copy?" Howell asked.

"The world is loud," Huntley read from the slide. "Your body is tired. You don't need to change your life; you just need to ReConnect. Bio-ionic support for the modern pace."

Howell nodded slowly. It sounded safe. It sounded like a solution that didn't require him to dismantle the building he was sitting in.

"And the barefoot walks?" one VitaGlobal executive asked. "The dirt?"

"We frame it as... unhygienic," Huntley said, rubbing the back of his neck where a tension headache was blooming. "Not because we hate nature. Because we value safety. Parasites. Glass. Tetanus. We remind them that civilisation was built for a reason. We remind them that shoes are progress." He looked at his polished brogues. He couldn't remember the last time his own feet had touched even remotely natural or outside. The thought made him feel incredibly heavy.

"We sell them the clean version, we act as the filter. That is our job. We take the raw, chaotic, dirty truth of the earth, which, let's face it, terrifies the average consumer and we refine it. We remove the risk. We remove the uncertainty. We put it in a blister pack that fits in a purse. We aren't stealing the cure, Marcus. We are civilising it. We are making it safe for the suburbs."

Huntley finished, his voice a whisper in the static-filled room.

"We aren't just selling a supplement, gentlemen. We are selling them the permission to keep wearing their shoes." The language was clean and perfectly crafted to make the consumer believe that the path to wellness lay in a branded box. Huntley continued on to explain the three-pronged attack,

"First, a deluge of digital ads and sponsored content across social media. Second, a network of paid health influencers and medical experts will appear on podcasts and news shows. They will subtly dismiss unproven, natural remedies as well-intentioned but dangerous. A trusted voice will reassure the public that real science was the only path to health. Finally, a series of articles will appear on what look like independent wellness blogs, all citing peer-reviewed studies and debunking the myths of unsubstantiated claims."

The impact was swift and insidious as the campaign spread across the public domain like wildfire.

On Jinjarli's online platforms, the heartfelt messages from individuals around the world were now interspersed with a new kind of comment,

"Looks nice, but where's the peer-reviewed data?" and "Don't risk your health with unproven fads. Talk to your doctor about real solutions." The voices were anonymous, but their language and talking points were eerily uniform. They were the ghosts of The Busguardian Group's campaign, a polished chorus of doubt.

. . . .

Late one evening, Jinjarli, Murray and Kirri sat in the studio. They were watching a television commercial. It was for a new product, an holistic supplement. The ad showed a person walking barefoot through a lush green field. The voiceover spoke of harnessing nature. The music was soothing and the message was a perfectly manufactured cure, a clean, sterile and profitable version of Jinjarli's own truth. The ad ended with a brand name and a clear instruction:

"Ask your doctor if ReConnect is right for you."

"They're not just trying to discredit me," Jinjarli said, his voice a low whisper. "They are trying to take the message and sell it back to the world as a pill." He was fighting against a piece of paper, a brand name and a billion-dollar market. The manufactured lie was out in the open and it was a formidable enemy. The digital world was no longer a place of hopeful connections; it was a battlefield of ideas. The campaign Jinjarli and his team had anticipated arrived not with a single broadcast, but as a relentless, suffocating tide. Social media platforms, the very tools Kirri had used to amplify their message, were now weaponised against them. Jinjarli, Murray and Kirri sat huddled over a laptop in the studio, a stark contrast to the quiet of the bush outside.

On the screen, the noise of doubt was a constant, flickering stream. Sleek, high-production videos from wellness influencers and paid health experts populated every feed. They didn't mention Jinjarli's name, but their message was a direct counterpoint to his truth. One video showed a woman smiling as she took a pill, a voiceover promising real science for real relief. The aesthetics, the soothing colours and the reassuring tone were all eerily familiar. Beneath every one of their posts, the comments section became a new front line. The hopeful messages from people sharing their stories were being buried under a flood of anonymous comments.

"Where's your data?" one wrote.

"This is not medicine. This is a scam," another chimed in. It wasn't organic criticism; it was an organised, coordinated effort, the bot-like language and talking points were a chilling testament to the campaign's scale. Murray, ever the pragmatist, was furious.

"We can fight back," he said, his fingers flying across the keyboard. "We can call them out." Kirri shook her head, her face pale in the light of the screen.

"We can't. They're too big. This isn't just about a few websites anymore. This is a multi-million dollar campaign. They're running ads that look like news and they're using influencers people trust." She pointed to a meme that was being shared widely, a simple graphic that used official-looking fonts to declare: Barefoot? That's old news. Real wellness is backed by science.

A deep, quiet frustration settled over Jinjarli. His truth was slow and quiet and felt. Their lie was fast, loud and everywhere. They weren't just attacking his art; they were attacking the very idea of a truth that wasn't for sale. How do you fight something that is designed to be seen everywhere, to be heard by everyone? He looked out the studio window at the bush, a silent, enduring presence against the digital noise. He felt the weight of it all, the fatigue that had been his long-time companion returned with a suffocating force. He was fighting a shadow and for every truth he told, they manufactured a hundred lies to drown it out.

. . . .

Across town, Dr Finch retreated to his home study; it was a fortress of order. Books were aligned by height, files were indexed by taxonomy and the only sound was the low, regular tick of an antique grandfather clock. It was here, late at night, that he dismantled the chaos Jinjarli had unleashed. He had Mick Davies' article, The Web of Ownership, printed out and pinned to a cork-board. Each paragraph was underlined, annotated with analytical precision: Correlation ≠ Causation, Conjecture, Libel. He dismissed the financial links as a journalist's manufactured narrative, an embarrassing but ultimately legal collection of prudent investment strategies that had been unfairly sensationalised. The attack on his reputation, though infuriating, was an expected casualty of the public sphere. But the anecdotal evidence was harder to dismiss. He had compiled a separate document: a clinical summary of the reported benefits from the barefoot walk. Improved sleep (8/10 subjects). Reduction in chronic, low-grade pain (7/10). He noted the high consistency, then aggressively wrote across the top: PLACEBO EFFECT (EXPECTED). Yet, the word EXPECTED felt brittle, a veneer over a growing unease. These were his patients, or at least, people like his patients. People he had failed to help with quantifiable, expensive solutions.

The logical fracture began with his wife, Hazel. For six months, she had been plagued by persistent migraines, a dull, crushing pressure that conventional pharmacology, prescribed by Dr Finch himself, had failed to touch. He had adjusted and re-adjusted her dosage, changed the compound and referred her to specialists. The failure was a professional bruise that had become a painful and personal wound. Just two nights before, Hazel had retreated to their bedroom, the blinds drawn tight. She was unable to tolerate even the soft glow of a digital screen. He had given her the maximum dose of Sumatriptan, a medication he knew was highly effective. It had done nothing. Standing at the foot of her bed, watching the grimace of pain pull at her face, he had felt a suffocating helplessness, a feeling entirely incompatible with his surgical training and clinical authority. Now, he looked from the page listing his patients' subjective reduction in pain back to the memory of Hazel's migraine. Jinjarli's claim was simple, free and utterly illogical. Yet, it was the one thing he hadn't tried. His mind became a battlefield.

"Unproven methodology," his training screamed. "Ethically indefensible to recommend. Empirical observation," a colder, smaller voice countered, reviewing the failures of the past six months. "Your current methodology has a 0% success rate with Hazel. Theirs has a reported 70% success rate with similar symptoms." He knew the danger. If he suggested such a thing, he would be betraying everything he stood for. He would be opening the door to the very quackery he publicly condemned.

He stood up, pacing the cool marble floor of his study. He walked to the window and looked out at the distant, silent earth, no longer seeing just inert rock and soil, but an unpredictable, living source of energy. His scepticism was firmly in place, but his certainty, his logical foundation, had cracked under the weight of his personal failure and a strange, compelling, measurable truth. The possibility was appalling, yet undeniable. He was standing on the precipice of a choice that could save his wife's pain, but ruin his life's work. The fear of discovery tasted like stale copper in Dr Finch's mouth.

His office was cold, the harsh fluorescent lights of the deserted hallway bleeding under his door. He wasn't using his clinic phone or his professional email. He was using a secure, encrypted personal channel, an old email address he hadn't touched in a decade, a necessary precaution against the watchful eyes of his colleagues on the regional health board and the deeper shadow of OmniCorp. He stared at the blank screen, the silence of the room amplifying the frantic drumbeat in his chest. This act was a betrayal of everything he had publicly championed. He began to type, forcing his request into the rigid, clinical language he knew best, attempting to cloak his personal desperation in academic rigour. He addressed the email to Professor Evelyn Reed.

Subject: Follow-up Inquiry: Bio-potential and Regional Health Protocols

Professor Reed,

Further to the ongoing public controversy in the Hammaholl region regarding unverified claims of physiological bio-potential transfer (earthing), I am tasked, in my capacity on the Regional Health Oversight Committee, with compiling a comprehensive review.

I find myself with a deficit of objective data concerning the mechanisms of alleged electron transfer and the purported reduction of body voltage in symptomatic individuals. Your area of expertise in biophysics is clearly relevant.

For the purposes of a complete and professionally rigorous review, which I believe you would agree is necessary to prevent the spread of harmful pseudoscience, I request access to any of your preliminary, unpublished baseline data and methodology concerning the aforementioned phenomena. Specifically, any data that correlates skin contact with the Earth's surface to measured physiological markers.

He read the email three times, tediously removing any word that hinted at personal curiosity or need. It was a perfect, cold request. He almost sent it. Then, he stopped. He thought of Hazel, of the relentless, unyielding pain and the bitter failure of every pain-killer he had prescribed. His professional armour cracked just enough to allow a single, almost imperceptible sliver of truth to slip through. He added one final sentence, burying it at the end,

While I remain committed to evidence-based protocol, I am also forced to acknowledge the current limitations of established pharmacological interventions in addressing highly persistent, subjective neurophysiological disorders. A comprehensive understanding is now imperative.

He hit send. The electronic pulse of the message leaving his laptop felt like a physical shock. He had done it. He had taken his first, terrifying step across the ideological dividing line, trading his professional certainty for a desperate, quiet plea for a truth he had spent his career denying. Now, all he could do was wait for the response from the scientist he had publicly opposed.

Three days later, a courier van delivered a large, sleek box to the Finch residence. It was not the mud of the lake; it was the Medi-Ground Sleep System, a top-of-the-line, TGA-approved medical device Alistair had ordered from a specialist supplier in Germany. It cost four thousand dollars. It promised Bio-compatible Electron Transfer via Silver-Thread Technology. It was safe. It was clean. It plugged into the ground port of the wall socket, theoretically bypassing the dirty electricity. Alistair set it up with surgical precision, smoothing the silver-threaded sheet over Hazel's mattress.

"It's a grounding system, Hazel," he explained that night, tucking the cord behind the nightstand. "It replicates the physics of the earth without the... variables. No parasites. No dirt. Pure science." Hazel lay down. She looked hopeful. Alistair watched the monitors. But within twenty minutes, she sat up, clawing at the sheet.

"It buzzes, Al," she whispered, rubbing her arms.

"It can't buzz, Hazel. It's passive."

"It feels like... like insects under the skin. It's too sharp. It's not quiet like the garden." She ripped the expensive sheet off the bed, her breathing shallow and panicked. "It feels like the wall socket is leaking into me. Take it away, Alistair. Please." Alistair stood there, holding the bundled, four-thousand-dollar sheet. He looked at the wall outlet. He realised with a sinking heart that the clean path was corrupted. The wiring in the house was full of dirty AC noise and the mat was just an antenna broadcasting that noise straight into his wife's nervous system. He couldn't plug her into the house. The house was the problem. If he wanted to stop the pain, he couldn't use a machine. He had to go to the source. The realisation made his stomach turn. He would have to take her to the dirt.

Chapter 17

Gurrong Dhang

The wound in the earthwork was healing, but it required more than just dirt to fix it. Jinjarli knelt in the centre of the giant sculpted figure, his hands submerged in a bucket of wet, red clay. He wasn't just patching a hole; he was performing a skin graft on the land itself. The defacement, the gouged lines, the black spray paint, had been scrubbed away days ago but the depression in the soil remained. It was a phantom ache in the landscape. Jinjarli worked rhythmically, pushing the new clay into the gash where the vandal's boot had stomped. He smoothed the edges, blending the fresh, bright ochre with the weathered, sun-baked soil of the original sculpture. It was physical, back-breaking work. His shoulders burned and the sweat dripped from his nose, turning the dust on the ground into tiny dark craters. He didn't hear Uncle Moray approach. The old man didn't walk so much as manifest, his footsteps syncing perfectly with the rustle of the wind in the kangaroo grass.

"You are working the clay too hard, fella," Moray's voice was a low rumble, like distant thunder. "You are trying to force it to forget." Jinjarli sat back on his heels, wiping a muddy forearm across his brow.

"I want it gone, Unc. Every time I look at this spot, I see that boot. I feel the hate." Moray stepped into the sculpture. He wasn't wearing shoes. His feet, broad and calloused, looked like they were carved from the same wood as the river red gums. He stopped at the edge of the patch Jinjarli was working on.

"The land doesn't forget," Moray said gently. "Look at the trees. See the burls? See the twisted branches where the storm broke them fifty years ago? They grew around the break. They became stronger at the break." He crouched down, his knees cracking audibly. He reached out and touched the seam where the new clay met the old.

"A scar is not a defect, Jinjarli. A scar is the skin remembering. It is the story of survival. If you smooth it out perfectly, you are lying about what happened here. You are denying the strength it took to heal." Jinjarli looked at the patch. He had been trying to make it invisible, to erase the violation.

"Leave a ridge," Moray advised, tracing a line with his thumb. "Let the texture remain. When people walk the songline, let their feet feel the bump. Let them ask, What happened here? You will tell them: They tried to break us and we grew back stronger." Jinjarli nodded slowly. He dipped his hands back into the bucket, but this time, he didn't smooth the clay to a mirror finish. He left the grain. He left the story.

Later, as the sun began to dip, casting long, bruised shadows across the lake, the two fellas sat on the bank together. The physical labour was done but the intellectual work was just beginning. Jinjarli had his notebook out, the one Professor Reed had given him, filled with grids and columns for data collection.

"Professor Reed needs protocols," Jinjarli said, tapping the pen against the paper. "She believes the multimeter readings but she needs a... a system. Something repeatable. She keeps asking about controlled variables." Uncle Moray chuckled, a dry sound like shifting gravel.

"Variables. The white man always wants to cut the world into little slices so he can eat it one bite at a time."

"It's how they understand, Unc. They need to know the method. How did the old people do it? Was it just walking? Was it sitting?" Moray looked out over the water, his eyes glazing over slightly as he drifted back through time.

"Walking was for maintenance," Moray said softly. "But when the sickness was deep... when the fever burned in the blood or the joints felt like they were filled with broken glass... we didn't just walk. We returned to the source. We used the Gurrong Dhang.

"The Healing Bed?" Jinjarli asked. He had heard the name but the practice had faded, one of the many things silenced by the missions and the hospitals.

"Let me tell you about Uncle Ray," Moray said, his voice taking on the cadence of a storyteller. "I was a boy, no bigger than Tilly. Ray had the bad blood. His legs were swollen like tree trunks, hot to the touch.

The white doctor at the mission gave him pills, but the swelling would not go down. Ray could not walk. His spirit was fading, getting ready to leave." Moray closed his eyes and the air around them seemed to shift. Jinjarli could almost smell the smoke of a fire that had burned sixty years ago.

"My grandfather took us out to the sandy rise near the river. They dug a pit. Not deep, just shallow, shaped like a man. They built a fire in that pit, a big, hot fire of River Red Gum, because that wood burns hot and holds the heat. They let it burn down until there was nothing but a bed of glowing orange coals, pulsing like a heart. Then," Moray continued, his hands moving in the air as if he were arranging the layers, "they scraped the coals out, leaving just the heat trapped in the blackened earth. They lined the pit with fresh, damp sand. Then came the leaves. Paperbark. Eucalyptus. Tea tree. Armfuls of them, green and oily. When the leaves hit the hot sand, they hissed. The steam rose up instantly, a thick, white cloud that smelled of medicine and earth." Jinjarli leaned in, captivated. He could imagine the scent, sharp, mentholated and earthy.

"They stripped Ray down and laid him in the pit, right on top of the steaming leaves. Then they covered him. More leaves on top, then possum skins, then a layer of sand on the very top to seal it all in. Only his face was showing." Moray opened his eyes, looking directly at Jinjarli.

"He stayed there all night. The heat from the earth opened his skin. The oil from the leaves entered his blood. But it was the grounding, Jinjarli. I know that now. He was buried in the earth's battery. The whole surface of his body, his back, his legs, his arms, were drinking in the electrons. The steam made the connection perfect. Water, heat, earth. He sweated out the sickness. It poured out of him like black water."

"And in the morning?" Jinjarli whispered.

"In the morning," Moray smiled, a flash of white teeth, "he walked home. The swelling was gone. The heat was gone. He lived another twenty years." Moray stood up and grabbed two shovels leaning against the trunk of a gum tree. He tossed one to Jinjarli.

"Dig." They moved to a sandy patch near the riverbank, where the sediment was loose and dry on top but held the memory of the river underneath. For twenty minutes, they worked in a rhythmic silence, digging a shallow trench about the length of a man and a foot deep. Jinjarli's muscles burned, the physical exertion flushing the lingering stress of the vandalism from his system.

"Good," Moray grunted. He gathered smooth river stones and placed them in a small fire Murray had started nearby. They waited until the stones were grey-hot, radiating a shimmering distortion in the air. With careful, practiced movements using two large sticks as tongs, Moray transferred the stones into the bottom of the pit, spacing them out like a spine.

"Now, the conductor," Moray instructed. He piled armfuls of fresh eucalyptus and tea tree branches onto the hot stones. The reaction was instant. Hiss-snap. The moisture in the leaves hit the heat and a plume of thick, white steam billowed up. The scent was overpowering, a sharp, medicinal punch of eucalyptus oil and damp earth that cleared Jinjarli's sinuses instantly.

"Get in," Moray ordered, pointing to the steaming pit. "On the hot stones." Jinjarli hesitated. at first, "The leaves protect you. The sand conducts. Get in before the spirit escapes."

Jinjarli stripped down to his shorts and lowered himself into the trench. He lay back on the bed of leaves. It was shockingly hot, but not burning. The steam enveloped him, opening every pore on his back. Moray and Murray worked quickly, shovelling warm sand over his legs, his torso, his arms, packing him tight until only his head remained free, resting on a folded towel. The sensation was terrifying at first, the weight of the earth pressing down, pinning him. Then, the shift happened. It started at his spine. The heat from the stones didn't just warm his skin; it seemed to dissolve the boundaries of his body. He felt the frantic, buzzing electrical noise in his nervous system, the residue of the cameras, the emails, the anger, all being pulled out of him. It was a physical drainage. He felt heavy. Unbelievably heavy. The earth was a giant magnet and he was just iron filings aligning to its field.

"Close your eyes," Moray's voice came from above, sounding miles away. "Don't think about the study. Just let the black water run out." Jinjarli drifted. He wasn't asleep, but he wasn't awake. He was suspended in the hum of the land. He felt the vibration of the river flowing nearby, not through his ears, but through the sand pressed against his ribs. When they dug him out an hour later, his skin was pink and steaming, slick with oil and sweat. He stood up and his knees didn't creak. The knot of tension that had lived between his shoulder blades since the vandalism was gone. He looked at his notebook lying on the grass. The words "Variable 1" and "Variable 2" looked small and silly compared to the immense, silent power he had just touched.

Silence settled over the lake. Jinjarli looked down at his notebook. The grid lines looked ridiculous now. How do you fit that into a spreadsheet?

"So," Jinjarli said, trying to bridge the gap. "We need to translate the Gurrong Dhang into… science." He clicked his pen. "Professor Reed wants to know the Duration of Treatment."

Moray shrugged.

"Until the spirit returns. Or until the stones get cold." Jinjarli couldn't help but laugh.

"I don't think Until stones get cold is a metric the medical journal will accept, Unc. Let's call it… 45 to 60 minutes? That's the heat retention of basalt."

"Write down 60 minutes," Moray agreed, a twinkle in his eye. "It sounds more important."

"And the Conductive Medium?" Jinjarli asked. "We can't use possum skins for the global study. Dr Kerma says we need a standardised material."

"Cotton," Moray said decisively. "Wet cotton sheets. It breathes like the skins. It holds the water like the leaves. If you dampen the sheet and lay it on the earth, then lay the person on the sheet… the current will flow." Jinjarli scribbled furiously. Protocol A, High-Surface Area Grounding. Subject supine. Interface, Dampened natural fibre. Substrate, Mineral-rich soil.

"What about the leaves?" Jinjarli asked. "The oils?"

"That is the pharmacology," Moray said. "The white coats love that part. For your study… for the volts… the leaves are just the conductor. The medicine is the charge. Let's keep it simple. Earth. Water. Body." Moray leaned over and tapped the notebook with a calloused finger.

"You see what we are doing, Jinjarli? We are taking a ceremony and turning it into a recipe. It is funny, eh? We have known the recipe for sixty-five thousand years. Now we have to write it down in their language so they don't starve."

"It's not just a recipe, Unc," Jinjarli said, looking at the scribbled translation of the sacred ritual into clinical terms. "It's a map. We're drawing a map for people who have lost their way home." Moray nodded, satisfied.

"Then make sure the map is clear. Because there are a lot of lost people out there." Jinjarli looked at the page. Variable 1: Soil Moisture Content (>15%). Variable 2: Skin Surface Area Contact (>40%). Variable 3: Duration (>45 mins). It looked cold. It looked clinical. But as he read it, he could still smell the steam of the tea tree leaves and feel the heat of the fire in the sand. The spirit was hiding in the variables, waiting to be discovered.

. . . .

The sun was high and bright over the Hammaholl Botanical Gardens, a manicured oasis of European order in the middle of the Australian landscape. Here, nature was tamed. The oaks and elms were planted in straight lines; the rose bushes were pruned to within an inch of their lives. It was the only kind of nature Alistair Finch truly felt comfortable in.

"I don't see why we're here, Al," Hazel said, adjusting her large sunglasses. She looked frail. The skin around her eyes was tight and bruised-looking, the lingering shadow of three days of migraine. "The light is aggressive today."

"Fresh air, Haze. Vitamin D. The psychiatrist suggested it might help with the serotonin levels," Alistair lied smoothly. He was carrying a picnic basket, an absurd prop he hadn't used in a decade. "We'll find a shade tree. Way in the back, away from the path."

They found a spot under a massive English Oak. The grass there was thick, lush and slightly damp from the sprinkler system. Alistair spread out the tartan blanket, synthetic fleece with a waterproof backing. He set it down carefully. Hazel sat down gingerly, rubbing her temples.

"It's thumping again. Just behind the left eye. I took the beta-blocker an hour ago, but..." She trailed off, the hopelessness evident in the slump of her shoulders. Alistair watched her. He felt the familiar knot of professional anxiety tighten in his chest. Then, he looked at the grass beyond the blanket. Green. Lush. Alive. He cleared his throat.

"Hazel, I... I read a paper recently. A study on circulation and inflammation."

"Another pill?" she asked wearily. "I can't take any more pills, Al. My stomach is in shreds."

"No. Not a pill. A... physical therapy." He tried to keep his voice casual, authoritative. "It involves direct contact with cooling surfaces to regulate the autonomic nervous system." She looked at him over her glasses.

"What does that mean?"

"It means," he hesitated, looking around to make sure no one from the Medical Board was walking their dog nearby. "It means I want you to take your shoes off and your socks. Put your feet on the grass." Hazel stared at him. "You want me to walk barefoot? Like a hippie? Alistair, there are ants. There's duck poo."

"Just sitting. Not walking. Just... put your feet on the ground. For twenty minutes. Humour me." she sighed, a sound of a long-suffering patience.

"Fine. If it stops you staring at me like I'm a clinical trial." She unlaced her expensive orthotic walking shoes. She peeled off her cotton socks. Her feet were pale, the skin thin and blue-veined. She stretched her toes, looking vulnerable. Slowly, she lowered them off the edge of the waterproof blanket. Her heels touched the soil. Her toes sank into the cool, green blades.

Alistair held his breath. He glanced at his watch. 2:14 PM. He wasn't looking at the scenery; he was watching her carotid artery, watching for the pulse rate. He was watching the tension in her trapezius muscles. He was observing.

"It's cold," Hazel said, shivering slightly. "But... wet."

"Is it unpleasant?"

"No," she said slowly. "It's... shocking. But in a good way." Alistair waited. One minute. Two minutes. He scanned the park, paranoid. If Ben Huntley or Dr Vance saw him here, treating his wife with dirt, his career would be over before the ink dried on the scandal sheet. This is research, he told himself. I am debunking it. Five minutes passed. A magpie warbled in the tree above them.

"Al," Hazel said softly.

"Yes? Is the pain worse? Do you need the sumatriptan?" He reached for his bag.

"No," she said. She wasn't looking at him. She was leaning back against the trunk of the oak tree, her eyes closed. Her face, usually pinched tight in a grimace of anticipated pain, had gone slack. The lines of tension around her mouth were smoothing out.

"It's... quiet," she whispered.

"The park?"

"No. The head. The thumping." She opened her eyes. They looked clearer, less glassy. "It feels like someone turned the volume knob down. It's still there, but it's... distant. Like it's draining out of my heels." Alistair felt a cold chill that had nothing to do with the breeze. He looked at her bare feet, buried in the grass. He thought of the diagrams Professor Reed had sent him, the electron flow, the discharge of static voltage.

"Scale of one to ten?" he asked, his voice tight. "It was an eight in the car." Hazel wiggled her toes in the dirt, a small, scandalous smile playing on her lips.

"Three. Maybe a two." Alistair looked at his watch. 2:24 PM. Ten minutes. Ten minutes of contact had done what six months of neurology appointments hadn't. He should have been relieved. He should have been overjoyed that his wife wasn't in agony. Instead, he felt a crushing wave of guilt. He looked at the waterproof blanket he was sitting on, insulating him from the ground. He looked at his own polished brogues, laced tight. He was the dead air. He was the circuit breaker, keeping the current from flowing. In that moment, he knew with a terrifying certainty, he couldn't keep this secret in the garden forever.

. . . .

     A fortnight later, the night before the big forum, the television in the Finch living room was a sixty-inch portal into the media storm. Alistair stood in the centre of the room, fully dressed in his suit, though it was 8:00 PM on a Sunday. He was rehearsing. On the coffee table lay the talking points provided by Ben Huntley and The Busguardian Group. They were printed on thick, glossy paper. Narrative Control. Safety First. The Danger of Unregulated Advice.

"We must consider the risks," Alistair said to the empty room, practicing his gravitas. "Public health cannot be guided by folklore. We need rigour. We need standards." He checked his reflection in the darkened window. He looked authoritative. He looked safe. But his eyes kept drifting to the expensive, discarded Medi-Ground box sitting in the corner, a reminder of his failure to synthesise a cure. "Standards," he repeated, trying to inject more conviction into the word. "The risk of infection from soil pathogens outweighs..."

The back door slid open. Alistair jumped, spinning around. Hazel walked in from the patio. The change in her over the last few weeks was startling.

She was wearing a loose linen dress, not the heavy, protective layers she usually favoured. Her hair was windblown and most damning of all, her feet were bare and stained with the dark, rich soil of the potting mix. She held a basket of herbs; rosemary, thyme, mint. The scent of them filled the sterile, air-conditioned room, becoming sharp and alive. She stopped when she saw him. She looked at the suit. She looked at the glossy papers on the coffee table. Then she looked at the television, which was playing a muted clip of Jinjarli standing on his stage.

"You're going on television again," Hazel said. It wasn't a question.

"It's a debate, Hazel. The Town Hall forum. It's important I represent the medical community. We have to warn people about the dangers of... of the environment." She walked over to the table and picked up the talking points. Her fingernails, usually manicured to perfection, had tiny crescents of dirt under them. Alistair stared at them. They fascinated him. They terrified him.

"Unsubstantiated claims," she read aloud. "Placebo effect. Dangerous implications of hygiene." She dropped the paper back onto the table. It made a sharp slap sound. She looked at him. Her eyes were hard.

"Is that what I am, Alistair? A placebo? Is the mud under my fingernails a danger?"

"Hazel, please. This is complicated. It's macro-economics, it's regulatory framework..."

"It's a lie," she said, her voice quiet but shaking. "It's a lie and you know it. Look at me, Al." She stepped closer. She smelled of the garden. She smelled of rain. "Three weeks. I haven't taken a migraine pill in three weeks. The machine you bought, hurt me. The pills you prescribed, hurt me. This," she pointed to the dirt on her feet, "healed me. You saw it happen. In the park. You measured my pulse. I saw you checking your watch, Alistair. I'm not stupid. You know exactly why I'm better." Alistair loosened his tie. The room felt suddenly stifling, the air conditioning unable to cope with the heat of the truth.

"I can't just... I can't just pivot, Haze. I'm the Chair of the Oversight Committee. I have a responsibility to the system."

"The system?" Hazel laughed, a bitter, hollow sound. "The system kept me in the dark for three years, Alistair. The system fed me pills that made my hair fall out and my stomach bleed. The system told me it was all in my head." She walked back to him, invading his personal space. She placed her hand on his chest. He could feel the warmth of it through his expensive shirt.

"You might lose your job, Alistair," she said softly. "But if you go on that stage and lie... if you try to take this away from people like me just to save your reputation... you will lose me."

She turned and walked out of the room. Alistair stood alone. He looked at the talking points: Safety First. He looked at the discarded medical device in the corner. He sat down heavily on the sofa, put his head in his hands and for the first time in his professional life, he didn't check the time. He just listened to the terrifying, liberating sound of the wind blowing through his house.

. . . .

The Hammaholl Town Hall, usually a dusty relic of civic pride smelling of floor wax and old timber, had been lobotomised. In its place stood a high-definition colosseum. Jinjarli stood just off-stage, watching a crew of technicians swarm over the stage. The transformation was total and aggressive. Thick coils of black cable snaked across the floorboards like invasive vines, taped down with aggressive strips of yellow-and-black hazard tape. The warm, forgiving incandescent lighting of the hall had been killed, replaced by towering rigs of LED floodlights that bathed the stage in a merciless, clinical white glare. It wasn't light designed to see by; it was light designed to interrogate.

"Mr Jinjarli? We need you in the chair," a young woman with a headset and a belt full of brushes said, grabbing his arm. She steered him toward a makeshift makeup station set up behind a black curtain. Jinjarli sat, feeling the heat of the mirror lights.

"Just a bit of powder," the woman said, attacking his face with a puff. "To kill the shine. The cameras hate sweat. And… oh." She paused, looking at his hands, which were stained with the red iron-oxide of the earthwork he had been repairing that morning. She reached for a wet wipe.

"Let me just clean that up for you."

"No." Jinjarli pulled his hand back sharply.

"Sir, it's going to look dirty on HD."

"It is dirt," Jinjarli said, his voice flat. "That's the point. I'm not going out there looking like a plastic doll. The dust stays." The woman looked at him, then at her supervisor, then shrugged.

"Suit yourself. But the lighting director isn't going to like the contrast." Jinjarli walked out to the stage. The heat was physical. The lights hummed with a high-pitched frequency that set his teeth on edge, the ultimate manifestation of the noise he had spent months fighting. He looked at the audience. It wasn't just locals anymore. The front rows were packed with journalists from the capital cities, typing on laptops, their faces illuminated by the blue glow of screens. Behind them sat the silent, sharp-suited allies of the pharmaceutical lobby, men who looked like they were carved from granite and dressed in Italian wool. And there, sitting at the end of the opposition table, was Dr Alistair Finch. He was disintegrating. On the outside, he was the picture of medical authority. His suit was pressed to a razor's edge, his tie was a sombre, trustworthy blue and his silver hair was perfectly styled. He sat with his hands clasped on the table, a statue of composure. Inside, his cardiovascular system was in revolt. His heart was hammering against his ribs, a frantic, irregular rhythm that he, as a doctor, would have diagnosed as acute stress-induced tachycardia. His palms were damp, leaving ghostly moist prints on the polished wood of the table. He resisted the urge to wipe them on his trousers. A trickle of sweat began to slide down his spine, cold and itching, but he didn't move. He couldn't.

The red tally light of the main camera was staring at him like a sniper's scope. Breathe, he told himself. Inhale for four. Hold for four. Exhale for four. It didn't work. The air in the room was too thin, burned up by the lights. He looked to his left. Ben Huntley, the strategist from The Busguardian Group, was checking his phone, looking bored. To his right, Dr Willow Vance from the NHOA was organising her notes, her face a mask of serene, regulatory arrogance. They looked so confident. So sure of the script.

Finch looked down at his own notes. They were typed bullet points on Placebo Effect and Dangers of Unregulated Therapy. They were the lies he was paid to tell. Then, a different image superimposed itself over the text. It was Hazel. This morning. He had woken up at 6:00 AM, the house silent. Usually, Hazel would be in bed until noon, hiding from the light, nursing the migraine that lived behind her eyes. The bed was empty. Panic flared, had she collapsed? He ran to the window and there she was. She was in the back garden. She was wearing her nightgown, the hem damp with dew. She was kneeling in the dirt, digging up carrots with her bare hands. She wasn't wearing gloves. She wasn't wearing shoes. He had watched, frozen, as she stood up, holding a muddy carrot to the sky. She had closed her eyes and inhaled, a smile spreading across her face, a smile he hadn't seen in three years. She looked radiant. She looked healed. When she came inside, her feet muddy and cold, he had asked,

"The head?"

"Gone," she had whispered, touching his cheek with a dirty finger. "It's just... quiet, Alistair. The earth took the noise away." Now, sitting under the brutal television lights, Finch felt the phantom touch of that muddy finger on his cheek. It burned hotter than the stage lights. He looked at his hands, clean, scrubbed, sterile. The hands of a man who prescribed pills that didn't work. I am a fraud, the thought tolled in his head like a bell. I am sitting here with the architects of the wall and my wife is in the garden tearing it down.

"We are live in five, four, three..." the floor manager counted down, pointing a finger at Mick Davies. Mick, looking surprisingly comfortable in a linen jacket, leaned into the microphone.

"Good evening, Australia. Tonight, from the regional town of Hammaholl, we discuss a profound question: Does healing require a prescription or a connection?" The debate began. Jinjarli spoke first. He stood planted on the stage floor, refusing to sit behind the table that hid his feet. He didn't look at the camera. He looked past the glare, searching for the faces of his mob in the back rows.

"My art is my truth," he said, his voice low and raspy, cutting through the polished audio mix. He held up the small, polished piece of Mount Scoria basalt. The camera zoomed in, catching the rough texture, the reality of the stone against the artificial set. "I am not selling a cure. I am sharing a realisation. The fatigue, the pain, it is the sound of our spirit being starved. My work is just a way of listening to the land's quiet, constant strength." Uncle Keerray followed. The lights seemed to dim around him, his presence creating its own gravity.

"The white coats tell you to stay off the ground," he rumbled. "We tell you the ground is your mother. It is your healer. When the scientists ask for proof, tell them to look at the persistence of my people. That is our proof. That is the unbroken songline." Then came Professor Reed. She brought the charts. She brought the graphs. She spoke the language that Finch understood, physics, voltage, electrons.

"We are not talking about magic," she stated, her voice sharp and professional, staring down Dr Vance. "We are talking about physics. Our data shows a measurable reduction in body voltage when grounded. The earth is a vast, natural circuit and our ancestors were simply better connected to the power source than we are today." Finch listened. He knew the physics. It made sense. It was elegant. It was true. And then, the tide turned. Mick Davies shifted the focus to the opposition.

"Dr Vance, the NHOA has issued warnings against this practice. Why?" Dr Willow Vance leaned into her microphone. She didn't raise her voice; she lowered the temperature of the room. She was the personification of the Nanny State.

"We commend the community for their passion," she began, her tone dripping with a condescension so refined it sounded like concern. "However, passion is not protocol. The NHOA is tasked with protecting citizens from unsubstantiated claims." She held up a thick binder. "The research presented by Professor Reed is preliminary and uncontrolled. We cannot endorse a practice based on anecdote. Furthermore," she pivoted to safety, the ultimate weapon, "encouraging the public to walk barefoot in urban environments risks infection, injury and parasites. We must promote treatments that are TGA-approved and risk-assessed. Anything less is a dereliction of duty." Ben Huntley, the pharmaceutical strategist, jumped in. He was smoother, slicker. He smiled a smile that cost more than Jinjarli's studio.

"We stand with Dr Finch," Huntley said, nodding toward Alistair. Finch actually flinched physically at the mention of his name. He felt nauseous.

"We fight complex ailments with complex solutions," Huntley continued, his voice soothing, hypnotic. "The pill you take is the result of billions of dollars of research. It is predictable. It is safe. Wellness is not a hobby. It is a serious scientific endeavour. Are we willing to gamble our nation's health on a feeling? On a romantic idea of the past?" He paused for effect. "When claims become extreme, they breed extremism. We urge the public to choose proven efficacy over unsubstantiated enthusiasms."

The silence that followed was heavy. It was the silence of a trap snapping shut. The audience was wavering. Vance and Huntley sounded so... reasonable. So safe. Finch sat there. The sweat was now running freely down his back. His heart was beating so hard he thought the microphone might pick it up. Proven efficacy, Huntley had said. Finch thought of the six months he had spent poisoning his wife with proven efficacy. He thought of her crying in the dark.

He thought of the silence of the garden this morning. He looked at the Redboulder Family Trust documents in his mind, the legacy of land ownership, of fencing the earth, of profiting from the separation. He was the heir to the wall. He looked at Jinjarli. The young man looked tired, dusty and dignified. He wasn't selling anything. He was just standing on the truth.

Finch gripped the edge of the table. His knuckles turned white. The logical part of his brain was screaming at him: Sit still. Say nothing. But the image of the useless 50mg syringe on his nightstand and the failed four-thousand-dollar mat, burned in his mind. The silence, Finch thought. I need the silence. The chair scraped back. Dr Alistair Finch rose. He walked toward the front of the stage, away from the safety of the table, away from Huntley and Vance. He moved with the rigid, fearful posture of a man walking into a firing squad.

"I was invited here tonight to represent the position of evidence-based medicine," Dr Finch began. His voice was shaking. He cleared his throat and started again, louder. "And I stand by that necessity." He paused.

The room was utterly silent. "However," he continued, turning his back on the camera to look at the audience. "Evidence takes many forms. The most damning evidence a physician can face is his own failure." He took a breath. It felt like inhaling fire. "I have listened to the consistency of the data presented here. But more importantly, I have reviewed my own case files. I treat patients with persistent, subjective neurophysiological disorders. Migraines. Chronic inflammation. Anxiety." He looked directly at Ben Huntley. "These are disorders that our established pharmacological protocols routinely fail to address. I have prescribed the pills. I have increased the dosages. And I have watched my patients, my own family, continue to suffer." A gasp went through the room. The admission of clinical failure was heresy.

"When the standard of care fails to cure," Finch stated, his voice gaining a sudden, powerful conviction, "and a non-invasive, free intervention succeeds... a physician's duty shifts. It ceases to be one of dismissal and becomes one of humility." He reached into his pocket. For a second, security tensed. Finch pulled out a small, orange prescription bottle. It was Sumatriptan. His wife's medication. The symbol of his inability to help her. He placed it gently on the table.

"I publicly retract my dismissal of the grounding hypothesis. Not because I understand the poetry of it, but because the pharmacology has failed us. I demand that independent research be commissioned immediately. We cannot hide behind safety when our own cures are not working." He looked at the camera one last time, his eyes wet but clear. "We have failed to heal them. We have no right to stop them from healing themselves." A gasp went through the room. Ben Huntley leaned forward, his polished facade cracking into a look of panicked disbelief. He made a gesture to the floor manager to cut the feed, but the cameras kept rolling.

"When the consistency of subjective improvement is coupled with the objective physics presented by Professor Reed," Finch stated, his voice gaining a sudden, powerful conviction, the tremors in his hands ceasing. He turned slowly to face Dr Vance and Ben Huntley. He looked them in the eye then he turned and walked back to his seat. He didn't sit down. He picked up his notes, the lies about the placebo effect and dropped them into the trash can by the moderator's desk. The Town Hall exploded. It wasn't applause; it was a roar of shock, a release of tension that shook the lighting rigs. Jinjarli and Professor Reed exchanged a look of stunned triumph. Dr Finch stood alone in the noise, his career in ruins, the cameras zooming in on his face and for the first time in years, if ever, the static in his head was gone. He was grounded.

Chapter 18

The Unbroken Frequency

The immediate aftermath of the televised forum was not a ripple; it was a societal earthquake. Dr Finch's Logical Confession, delivered with the raw vulnerability of a man dismantling his own life on live television, was the moment of conversion for the nation. The highly-regarded medical authority, the living embodiment of the system, had shattered the professional façade of dismissal. A man who had everything to lose had just validated Jinjarli's truth. The digital static of the corporate PR campaign, the bots, the paid influencers, the slick ReConnect ads, were instantly overwhelmed by an organic, viral surge of support.

In his studio, Jinjarli sat with Kirri and Murray, watching in stunned silence as the term #SicknessOfDisconnection, trended number one across Australia, then the UK, then Canada. But the real change wasn't online. It was in living rooms.

In a cramped apartment in suburban Melbourne, Sarah, a junior lawyer, sat on her couch, her laptop open on her knees. She had been working for twelve hours straight, her shoulders tight knots of tension, her eyes burning from the screen glare. She was watching the replay of the forum on her phone. She watched Dr Finch put the pill bottle on the table. She heard him talk about the failure of his own medicine. She looked down at her own feet, encased in thick wool socks. Her apartment floor was polished concrete, trendy, cold and insulated. She felt a sudden, overwhelming urge to escape it.

"Tom," she called out to her partner, who was doom-scrolling in the kitchen. "We're going out."

"It's 9:30 on a Tuesday," Tom yelled back. "Where?"

"To the park." Ten minutes later, they were standing on the edge of the local oval. The grass was damp with the evening dew, reflecting the orange glow of the streetlights. It was cold.

"This is stupid," Tom grunted, shivering in his jacket. "We're going to get sick." Sarah didn't answer. She untied her trainers and kicked them off. She peeled off her socks. She stepped onto the grass. The cold was a shock. But then, a second sensation followed. It was a subtle tingle that started in her arches and travelled up her shins. The relentless buzzing in her head, the echo of emails and deadlines, seemed to drop a decibel. The tightness between her shoulder blades released just a fraction. She closed her eyes and took a deep breath of the cold night air. It smelled of wet soil and cut grass.

"Sarah?" Tom asked, his voice softer.

"Just... wait," she whispered. She wiggled her toes into the damp earth. She felt tethered. She felt real. Tom watched her for a minute. Then, silently, he bent down and started unlacing his boots.

All over the country, the scene was repeating. Office workers in Sydney's Barangaroo corporate park were slipping off their loafers at lunch and standing on the small patches of ornamental lawn. Families picnicking in Brisbane's botanic gardens were encouraging their kids to run barefoot. The contrast between the slick, manufactured lie of the ReConnect Initiative and the raw, undeniable simplicity of the barefoot walkers was too big to ignore. Public opinion didn't just shift; it swung violently. The narrative was no longer about a fringe theory; it was about a powerful institution covering up a free cure.

The political and professional fallout was immediate and severe. Mick Davies' article, The Web of Ownership, which had been dismissed by Ben Huntley as sensationalist, was now treated as a foundational document. Major national news organisations, which had initially sent junior reporters to Hammaholl, now launched full-scale investigative teams. The spotlight was aimed squarely at the National Health Oversight Agency (NHOA) and its leadership. Within forty-eight hours, an independent Member of Parliament, citing Dr Finch's testimony and Mick's documented financial links, formally called for a Parliamentary Inquiry into the NHOA's regulatory practices. The pressure on Dr Vance and Ben Huntley became insurmountable. Corporate allies began distancing themselves from the NHOA, fearing the spread of financial infection. The truth had become a public liability. The national consensus was clear, the system that had been designed to protect the public had, in fact, protected corporate profit.

Jinjarli, Uncle Keerray and Professor Reed were no longer seen as outsiders fighting a losing battle; they were seen as truth-tellers providing the evidence for a national reckoning. The forces of justice had joined their side and the final confrontation with the architects of the disconnection was now inevitable. With the public mandate clear, the focus shifted to securing the resources needed to win the scientific war. Professor Evelyn Reed had been working for weeks on securing the massive financial resources required to execute a rigorous, global study that would stand against the billions wielded by OmniCorp. The pivotal meeting took place on a secure video line. Jinjarli was in his studio, Murray and Kirri beside him. Professor Reed was in her lab. On the other side of the call were three men in expensive suits, sitting around a polished boardroom table in Zurich. They were representatives of a major European philanthropic foundation focused on public health.

"Gentlemen," Professor Reed began, her tone crisp and authoritative. "The landscape has fundamentally shifted. Dr Finch's testimony has created a vacuum of credibility in the current regulatory framework. The public is demanding independent verification." She laid out the proposal, a multi-national, double-blind study involving thousands of participants, measuring inflammatory markers, cortisol levels and sleep quality, all correlated with precise grounding protocols. The man in the centre, a silver-haired director named Herr Weber, nodded slowly.

"The proposal is robust, Professor Reed. The public interest is undeniable. We are prepared to offer the full seed funding of five million Euros." Jinjarli felt a jolt. Five million. It was a number he couldn't' even comprehend.

"However," Weber continued, leaning forward, "given the scale of the investment, the foundation requires certain... assurances. We would need to appoint a steering committee to oversee the data collection protocols. Naturally, the intellectual property resulting from the study, any patents for therapeutic devices or methodologies, would be shared with the foundation." Professor Reed went very still. Jinjarli felt a cold prickle of recognition. He had seen this move before. It was the white man arriving with a contract.

"Herr Weber," Reed said, her voice dropping to a dangerous chill. "Let us be clear on what we are studying. We are not testing a new drug. We are validating a sixty-five-thousand-year-old knowledge system." She gestured to Jinjarli on the screen. "The protocols, the healing beds, the use of basalt, the understanding of the conductive nature of water, these are not methodologies I invented in a lab. They are the cultural intellectual property of the Gundarra people. They are not for sale and they are certainly not patentable by a European foundation." Weber looked taken aback.

"Professor, we are simply talking about standard return on investment. If this research leads to a new type of conductive mattress, for example…"

"Then that mattress will be based on stolen knowledge," Jinjarli spoke up, his voice vibrating through the microphone. The room in Zurich went silent. "I appreciate your money, sir," Jinjarli continued, looking directly into the camera. "But my people have spent two centuries having our land, our children and our stories stolen. We are not going to let you take our healing, too. You want to fund the truth? Good. But the truth belongs to the earth and the knowledge belongs to its custodians." He paused, letting the weight of his words land.

"You fund the study because it's the right thing to do. Not because you want to own the result. The data will be open source. Free for the world and the Gundarra people will retain full rights to their traditional knowledge. Those are the conditions." Weber exchanged a glance with his colleagues. There was a tense, hushed discussion in German. Jinjarli held his breath. He was risking five million euros on a principle.

Finally, Weber turned back to the camera. He looked at Jinjarli with a new expression, not just of a financier, but of a man recognising power.

"Very well, Mr Jinjarli," Weber said quietly. "We accept your terms. The foundation will fund the study as a public good. The data will be open. The knowledge remains yours." Jinjarli let out a breath he felt he'd been holding since 1788.

"The total is significant enough to launch the full-scale study we designed," Professor Reed confirmed, a rare smile breaking through her professional demeanour. "It means we can acquire the high-precision body voltage meters, thermal imaging equipment and crucially, support the Indigenous-led qualitative studies." A portion of the funds were directly allocated to the Gundarra community, covering all resources required for Uncle Moray and Auntie Tarni's work.

"The multimeter, the ochre... they were a whisper," Jinjarli said, looking at the screen full of international faces. "Now, we have the resources to make the songline a roar."

With the funding secured, Jinjarli's focus shifted inward. The success of the global study depended not just on equipment, but on trust and understanding within his own community. The most vital part of the unbroken songline was ensuring the next generation could carry the melody. The setting for the lessons was the repaired earthwork near Lake Lumina. It was a tangible textbook, its ochre lines illustrating the very principles they were discussing. A small group of young fellas from the Gundarra mob, including Tilly, gathered around Jinjarli, their eyes holding a mix of digital-age curiosity and ancestral reverence.

Jinjarli began the lesson not with the multimeter, but with the story of the Gurrong Dhang, the healing earth pits.

"Our old people didn't need a yellow box to tell them the earth was alive," he explained, his bare feet sinking into the cool, rich soil. "They learned through feeling. When sickness came, they practiced, Returning to Source, lying directly on the land. Uncle Keerray taught me that this was their protocol for the sickness of disconnection." He emphasised that their ancestors were not just surviving; they were practicing empirical science.

"The ancient wisdom is the truth, but the multimeter is the proof," he said. "You must learn to speak both languages." Jinjarli guided them through simple exercises, asking them to sit and stand on different textures, the warm, dry sand; the cool, damp mud near the lake; the rough, conductive basalt. He asked them to report not on data, but on sensation: the subtle cooling of the skin, the easing of tension, the quiet strength that flowed up from the ground. Murray, the practical mind, assisted by demonstrating the principles. Jinjarli would place the probe on his ankle and Tilly would hold the multimeter, watching the numbers jump from 0.01 volts on the dry track to 0.07 volts on the damp earth. This simple act translated the spiritual into the quantifiable.

"The number isn't the healing," Jinjarli taught them. "The number is just the map showing you the direction to the healing." The lesson was infused with the weight of responsibility. Jinjarli spoke of the vandalism, of Dr Finch's initial denial and of the corporate giants who feared a free cure. He told them that their knowledge was a threat to a multi-billion-dollar industry and that their duty was now two-fold, to protect the land and to protect the truth.

Tilly, ever eager, grasped the concept instantly. She stood on a rubber mat, watching the meter read zero. Then she stepped onto the earth, her face lighting up as the numbers climbed.

"So the shoes are the wall," she stated. "And the numbers are the secret knock?" Jinjarli smiled, placing a hand on her shoulder.

"Yes, Tilly. The numbers are the secret knock. But the Songline is the song that's waiting on the other side." By the end of the day, the young ones were no longer just curious onlookers. They were the new custodians of the pulse, carrying the ancient wisdom in their hearts and the language of modern proof on their lips. They understood that the future of their community's health and perhaps the health of the disconnected modern world, depended on their ability to keep the Songline strong.

As the sun went down, after the young ones had gone back to their homes, Jinjarli entered Elder Keerray's hut. The fire was reduced to a deep, steady bed of glowing coals. The quiet noise of the night outside was a world away from the digital static and the professional feuds that dominated Jinjarli's days.

"You wanted to see me, Unc?" Jinjarli asked as he sat across from his Elder, the faint scent of smoke a comforting presence. Keerray studied Jinjarli, his gaze penetrating and warm. He didn't ask about the five million euros or the ongoing NHOA investigations. He looked past the battles and focused on the spirit.

"You have fought a great war, child," Keerray began, his voice low and rich, holding the weight of countless seasons. "A war waged with numbers and with paint. You faced the men in the white coats and you faced the men with the shadows, those who wished to erase your truth." He reached out and gently placed his gnarled hand over Jinjarli's ochre-stained one. "But your greatest victory was not over the doctor or the men who soiled the ground. Your victory was the courage you showed in standing at the centre of the bridge. You dared to take the ancient pulse and translate it into a language they could not dismiss." Keerray spoke of the young ones, Tilly and the others, learning the Gurrong Dhang protocols, measuring the volts with the multimeter.

"They are no longer just walking on the land; they are listening to it again. You have turned a forgotten wisdom into a vital instruction for them." He paused, a grand and resonant pride settling in his eyes. "For two hundred and thirty-five years, they tried to tell us the land was silent. They told us our way was a weakness. They built walls of concrete and silence between us and our Mother Earth. The Songline," he affirmed, his voice growing stronger, "was not broken. It was just sung softly, waiting for a clear voice. You, Jinjarli, have given it that volume." The Elder sighed, a sound of deep, ancient satisfaction.

"This knowledge, the truth of the unbroken connection, is the greatest inheritance of our people. I was afraid it would be lost forever in the noise of the modern world. Now, it is safe. Now, it is armed with the science they demand and it is being carried by the young fellas. You have healed a wound not just in your own body but in the body of our memory." He raised his hand and gently touched Jinjarli's forehead in a quiet blessing.

"I have never been more proud. Go now. Fight your final battles. You carry the wisdom of sixty-five thousand years in your hands. You are the resurgence, my boy.

Chapter 19

The Map is Home

Years slipped into the past, taking with them the heat of the town hall debates and the digital static of the corporate war. The victory, forged in Jinjarli's backyard, had spread outward like ripples in the lake, but its source remained sacred. The earthwork near Lake Lumina was no longer a symbol of controversy; it was a testament to Indigenous perseverance to prove unity. It had been meticulously maintained, its ochre lines refreshed each season and was now a protected, sacred site, a living songline that drew visitors from across the country, even from across the globe. They came to feel the pulse of Gundarra Country.

The Global Bio-Electrics Consortium, under the leadership of Professor Evelyn Reed and Dr Amaria Kerma, had successfully published their data in the world's leading medical journals. The combined empirical rigour of their study, measuring body voltage reduction alongside Elder Moray's meticulous qualitative tracking of the Gurrong Dhang protocols, was undeniable. The pivotal moment had come in Geneva. Dr Kerma, now independent and formidable, stood at a massive conference podium, commanding the attention of thousands of white-coated physicians who had once dismissed her work as inconvenient noise. She clicked a button, projecting a graph that showed the divergence of two lines: the placebo group's consistent inflammation markers and the rapidly declining markers of the Gurrong Dhang intervention group.

"For decades, we sought a complex, patented solution to chronic inflammation," Kerma stated, her voice quiet but ringing with authority. "The truth, as taught by the Gundarra people, was simply a charge transfer. The solution was free."

The published conclusion, now quoted in medical texts worldwide, validated the ancient wisdom with clinical certainty: "The consistent physiological coupling of the human body to the negative electrical charge of the Earth's surface represents a robust, first-line, non-pharmacological intervention for the regulation of autonomic nervous system function and the reduction of inflammatory cytokines." Grounding, or Earthing, was no longer a fringe theory; it was a first-line, physician-recommended intervention for chronic inflammation, stress and sleep disorders. The simple act of connecting with the earth had been scientifically validated as a powerful, free therapy.

The initial scepticism had fractured. The NHOA scandal led to sweeping ethical reforms across Australia's health oversight bodies. New legislation mandated the inclusion of accessible, conductive green spaces in all major urban developments and building codes began to favour materials that maintained the electrical connection to the earth, reversing decades of insulating architecture. The most profound change was visible on the street, across Australia and globally. The Barefoot March had become a quiet cultural revolution. People walked barefoot in city parks, on beaches and even in designated public grounding areas.

In the city square of Hammaholl, the local council had commissioned an award-winning community centre. It wasn't just beautiful; it was a functional monument to the truth. The main entrance plaza was paved with polished basalt stones interlaced with fine copper threading, a deliberate conductive path. This practical Songline guided people toward a large, open-air earth patio where children played, their bare skin pressed against the living ground. The image of the rubber-soled shoe, the symbol of the wall, had become an ironic marker of the old, disconnected way of life.

Meanwhile, the campaign Jinjarli fought against had dissolved into failure. The slickly branded ReConnect Initiative pills, the expensive lie intended to package the free cure, sat on dusty clearance shelves in defunct pharmacies. Jinjarli had visited one once, finding a solitary, forlorn box marked down by 90%. The pill, designed to address the sickness of disconnection, had been rendered obsolete by the earth itself.

Jinjarli, now much older, his hair flecked with grey, stood on the rise overlooking the earthwork. He was no longer just an artist; he was an elder and cultural ambassador. His art, a fusion of ochre-stained canvases and scientific schematics, was displayed in museums everywhere, a vivid symbol of the truth that healed the world. Uncle Keerray's wisdom was now quoted in medical journals worldwide, his simple phrase, sickness of disconnection, having become the diagnostic term for modern malaise.

Elder Moray and Auntie Tarni ran the Gundarra Healing Initiative, sharing the traditional protocols with practitioners globally, ensuring the knowledge was taught with respect and cultural integrity. In a sleek, sunlight-drenched office building built from reclaimed wood and conductive flooring, Murray and Kirri managed the Unbroken Songlines Global Data Exchange. They were still digital warriors, but their war was won, replaced by a lifelong mission of guarding the data. Kirri worked swiftly, programming new security algorithms, while Murray sat nearby. On his desk, nestled between twin high-resolution monitors, was the dusty, yellow multimeter. It was the fragile, crucial artefact that had bridged the divide.

Across town, Dr Alistair Finch, having lost his prestigious position and finding his conscience, now ran a small, highly respected integrative wellness clinic. His uniform was soft, 321 breathable linen and his first question to every patient wasn't about symptoms, but environment. In his consultation room, he looked at a middle-aged woman struggling with chronic fatigue.

"We can certainly discuss supplements," Finch said, his voice softer, patient. "But first, tell me: How long did you spend on the earth this week?" His wife, Hazel, was migraine-free. That physical peace was etched onto her face, a profound contrast to the tight mask of pain Jinjarli remembered. She often volunteered at a local community garden, working the soil with her bare hands, feeling the strength flow up her arms. They had found a peace his rigid life could never offer him.

The End

Acknowledgements

Writing this book was a journey from the "Marble" back to the "Mud," and I didn't walk the track alone. First and foremost, to my seven sons and two grand babies. You are my greatest teachers in resilience, my loudest cheerleaders, and the very reason I strive to keep our songlines unbroken. Thank you for the chaos, the laughter and for keeping me grounded every single day. To my Mum, your strength through your own battles has been a lighthouse for me. This book carries your spirit in every chapter. A deep and respectful thank you to the Gunditjmara people, thank you for allowing me to explore your profound wisdom. To my friends, for believing in the "Barefoot Prophet" before the rest of the world caught on. Finally, to the land itself—for the 0.03-volt whispers and the lakeside strength. Thank you for always being there to catch us when we finally decide to take off our shoes.

About the Author

Nikkie Maud is a creative powerhouse who thrives where the tangible meets the transcendent. A chef by trade, an artist by instinct, and a storyteller by heart, Nikkie doesn't just write—she brews, paints, and builds worlds. Based in the rugged, beautiful landscape of Hamilton, Victoria, she brings a chef's "secret sauce" precision and an artist's flair to everything she touches.

At the very centre of Nikkie's world is her role as a mother to seven sons and two grand babies. Living in a house powered by that much "boy energy" is a high-octane masterclass in resilience and love. This beautiful, bustling reality is what keeps her "barefoot" philosophy grounded; she knows the best lessons aren't found on a polished pedestal, but right there in the mud of real life.

Nikkie's creative voice is a vibrant tribute to Aboriginal and Torres Strait Islander histories, with a deep, soulful focus on the Gunditjmara people and the healing frequencies of the land. She is on a mission to translate ancient wisdom into a modern language of healing, helping a disconnected world kick off its shoes and reconnect with the Earth.

Whether she's rewiring an e-bike, designing a soul-mapping tattoo, creating for nikkieMAUDdesign or finalising a manuscript for Keystrokes by MAUD, Nikkie is a force of nature. She stands as living proof that when you mix a bit of grit with a whole lot of soul, you can bridge the gap between the clinical "Marble" and the sacred, life-giving "Mud."

Get Grounded

A simple, upbeat guide for readers who finished the book and want to try earthing for themselves.

- Step 1: Find a patch of "Source"—damp grass, beach sand, or rich soil.

- Step 2: Ditch the "rubber coffins" (your shoes) for at least 20 minutes.

- Step 3: Breathe. Let the Earth's 0.03-volt "secret knock" do the rest.

<u>Also by Nikkie Maud</u>

- Echoes of Song: A short story exploring deep connection.

- Spark to Story: The Alchemist's Guide to Writing: Your online course for fellow creators.

- A Day in the Life of Silly Tilly: A children's book series about an American Bulldog and her crazy adventures

- nikkieMAUDdesign - is a multidisciplinary creative engine featuring a gallery for completed projects, 'Illume' art school, a soulful blog, and a curated shop where ancestral storytelling meets modern trade

- Keystrokes by MAUD - is a boutique independent publishing imprint that serves as the narrative heart of your creative ecosystem, dedicated to sharing grounded stories and metaphysical truths that bridge the gap between ancient songlines and the modern world.

- …..and much more!

A Special Invitation

The story doesn't have to end at the final page. If you felt the "secret knock" of the Earth while reading, I invite you to step into the illume Art School & Gallery.

Located within the nikkieMAUDdesign ecosystem, illume is a space dedicated to shedding the "Marble" and embracing the "Mud." Whether you are looking to explore our gallery of ochre-stained works, shop for grounded products, or join a workshop to find your own creative frequency, there is a place for you here.

Visit us at www.nikkieMAUDdesign.com to read the blog, view the latest collections, and begin your own journey back to Source.